Dark Knights of the Soul

Dark Knights of the Soul

JEREMY SIMPSON

QUARTET

First published in 2010 by
Quartet Books Limited
A member of the Namara Group
27 Goodge Street, London W1T 2LD

A catalogue record for this book
is available from the British Library

ISBN   978 0 7043 7189 7

Typeset by Antony Gray
Printed and bound in Great Britain by
T J International Ltd, Padstow, Cornwall

NORMALLY CHARLOTTE was a calm Cambridge historian, but sitting next to Nicholas, a fellow academic, she was twisting a damp handkerchief as she questioned him as he drove like a maniac towards the Swiss/German border. She was trembling, trying to get the words out.

'I just can't grasp what's happened – you're telling me that you and Theo put the Grand Master's mistress in a coffin, having removed Sergeant Margaret who is now groaning on the back seat, and that this coffin is due to be buried in the Templar courtyard as the sun sets this evening. Nicholas, this is unbelievable! To think that just two hours ago Kirsten and I were packing books in the castle library when you burst in looking like Hamlet's ghost, telling us to get out as our lives are in danger. No explanation, just that the Templars will do the killing! My God Nicholas, this is too much to take in.' Charlotte dabbed her eyes with an already soggy hanky and looked out of the window. She saw nothing of the countryside rushing by. 'And then when we get to the hotel in Zurzach to collect our bags, we've got this Templar girl, Maggie, hidden in the boot. Nicholas, promise me that there's a way out of this nightmare ... '

Nicholas touched Charlotte's arm, unable to hide his shaking hand.

'Trust me, my love. Theo explained it all on the phone to Colonel Baker and he's sending a plane to Germany to get us out.'

'Some comfort! We've got to get there first.'

A groan came from the girl lying on the back seat of the car. She was dressed in a silver lurex long dress, leather belted and with a red Templar cross emblazoned on it. Her neck was red and bruised.

They came to the road leading to the frontier crossing at Koblenz and found the traffic crawling slowly. In front of them their friend Theo, a Greek-American Harvard academic, lowered his window and waved. With him was an American librarian, Kirsten.

The border controls over the Rhine at Koblenz are perfunctory. However on this June day, the normal easy flow of traffic had turned into a slow-moving tide as the border police on the Swiss side were examining every car and passport. For most of the drivers the result was a heightening of their blood pressure or the drumming of fat fingers on steering wheels. However for Nicholas, his hands trembled violently as he rested them from the steering wheel of their car. In addition to the horror of the coffin, the knowledge he carried was so overwhelming – knowledge gleaned in the crypt chapel below the Templar Church.

Charlotte interrupted his thoughts. 'How do we get out of this if the police detain us at the border?'

Nicholas shook his head. 'I don't think what happened will have been discovered yet.'

The slow-moving traffic stopped. Theo got out of his car in front of them and came back to them and leant through the window.

'They can't have found that witch in the coffin yet. We must just keep our nerve and once in Germany we go like hell to the airport at Blumberg where Colonel Baker is sending a plane.'

Theo had telephoned before they left the hotel and told the Colonel as much as he could about what they had learnt in the crypt under the Templar Church in the castle. He had also informed him about removing Maggie from the coffin and replacing her with the Grand Master's mistress. Colonel Baker said he would ring the Grand Master and tell him his girlfriend was in the coffin instead of Maggie, but that he would first wait to hear that they had got on board the plane.

Theo turned to look at the Swiss girl on the back seat.

'How is Maggie? It must be hot in that ridiculous Templar gear.'

Maggie smiled wanly and massaged the red weal around her neck.

Theo stood up and looked towards the bridge to see what was happening. He froze at what he saw – approaching them slowly was the immense shape of a Maybach limousine. It had a Templar flag fluttering on the top of its radiator and was preceded by two motor cycle outriders. They looked like leather-clad police, all in black save for red Templar crosses on their uniforms. Theo registered the implications of this approaching cavalcade. He opened the back door of Nicholas's car and jumped in and pushed the Swiss girl down on the floor behind the front seats.

'If it's who I think it is we are dead meat if they see Maggie. For Christ's sake look down.'

As the immense limousine glided past, they glimpsed the Grand Master of the renascent Templar Order looking straight ahead in the back of the limousine. He was on his way to an interment ceremony of the coffin that was supposed to contain the body of Maggie. As the limousine passed by, the cars behind them started to sound their horns; the traffic was moving again in front of them. Theo jumped out and returned to Kirsten in the other car.

'See you in Germany. We'll keep together until the first café we find and then we can stop and agree our next move. Good luck.'

Nicholas eased the car forward. They could now see the police examining passports and cars. The tension in the car was palpable. The last thing that was needed was for Maggie to sit forward and say in a strangled voice, 'Oh my God! I don't have my passport – the Templars have it!'

Charlotte groaned. 'This is a nightmare. Why the hell did we accept those bloody invitations?'

Nicholas remembered their excitement when they had received them on Valentine's Day earlier that year.

2

St Valentine's Day had started well for Nicholas Travers, a young professor at Michaelhouse College, Cambridge.

He had three Valentine cards and a large, gold-embossed invitation to attend a Templar seminar in a luxury hotel outside Zurich. He had placed these on the Tudor stone fireplace in the set of rooms assigned him in the College for his tutorials. A gas log fire cleverly incorporated into the grate was providing warmth; there had been a hard frost overnight. Outside the sun was appearing over the roof of the College in an azure sky, and whitened grass in the courtyard was beginning to melt and show green patches. A full moon was sulking in the sky as it faded in the sun's increasing brightness.

Nicholas opened the Valentine cards one by one and he arranged them in order of importance. First was one from a young don at Newnham. It was of traditional Victorian design and inside was a drawing of a fox, trailing a line of kisses and signed, 'Your Vixen'. He knew it was from the current love of his life, one Charlotte Fox-Travers. Nicholas experienced the poetic reaction of feeling weak at the knees as he counted the kisses on the card.

Next was a Valentine from his mother. It was a reproduction of the Great War recruiting poster of Kitchener pointing at potential conscripts to the army. The message had been changed from, 'Your country needs You', to 'Marriage needs You'. He knew it was from his mother; she was longing for him to marry and provide her with grandchildren. She hadn't even bothered to get it posted away from Bath where she lived, filling her widowhood hours with bridge and good works.

The third card was signed with five hearts and the message, *'Love your lectures and supervisions, Love you Tortoise'*. He tried to guess which of the girls who attended his lectures and supervisions might be responsible. He knew he was nick-named Tortoise because he affectedly wore a pair of old horn-rimmed spectacles and walked slowly up and down when lecturing. The nickname had its origin from Lewis Carroll's character Tortoise because he 'taught us'. Finally he turned his attention to the invitation. It read:

The Knights of the Temple of Solomon request the
pleasure of your company at a seminar entitled
'The Templars' Rebirth' to be held at
the Dolder Grand Hotel, Zurich.
From 18.00 hours Friday March 26th
to 16.00 hours Sunday March 28th.
RSVP The Guest Master,
The Temple, Zurzach, Switzerland.

With this invitation was a single piece of expensive white notepaper. On it in fine italic was written:

All expenses of travel and accommodation provided.

And finally,

We invite you to meet the Grand Master at a special symposium after the seminar.

This piece of paper was embossed with the heraldic badge of twelfth-century Knights Templars showing two riders on one horse.

Nicholas was intrigued to be asked to a special gathering after the main event and liked the idea of it being described as a symposium – the Greek description of a drinking party. He was flattered that he had been invited. Two years ago he had a minor success when his thesis for his doctorate on

'The End of the Templars' had been published by the Cambridge University Press. It had received good reviews, but because of its specialised nature, modest sales. He had also had an article in *History Today* the previous autumn on the mystery of the escape of the Templar ships and possibly some of their treasure from La Rochelle, when the majority of the Order was being arrested in 1306 by the forces of the French King, Philip the Fair.

Nicholas regarded the idea of a rebirth with some scepticism. There had been numerous attempts in previous times to create new orders of the Knights Templars. Emperor Napoleon III of France had supported the creation of a nineteenth-century Order of the Temple, dedicated to acts of charity, but it did not survive the Great War. In the 1930s there was a modern revival and several countries have priories allied tenuously to each other and calling themselves the Supreme Military Order of the Temple of Jerusalem: their members engage in charitable work with no military ambitions and claim to be ecumenical in spirit, but enjoy bogus titles for themselves and dress up in robes at various functions. However, the so-called New Templar Order had been in the news after the Twin Towers tragedy in New York, in that it appeared to be growing fast and was rumoured to be largely funded by members of the American far right, plus money from extreme evangelical churches. Part of its success was said to be due to the fact that the Grand Master had appeared on American television and apparently foretold the 9/11 tragedy six months before. It was obviously financially successful to be hosting a gathering in one of Switzerland's most expensive hotels.

This hotel was of great interest to Nicholas as his university earnings precluded many visits to luxury hotels. However he was addicted to them and twice a year he would select such a hotel and take a short visit, funded by income from a grandfather's legacy. He kept an extensive collection of brochures and guides, mostly in a small cottage where he lived in Madingley, a village outside Cambridge. A smaller number of guides were in the bookshelf in his college rooms, including an old copy of *The Leading Hotels of the World*. He picked it up and read the description of the Dolder Grand.

Zurich's only city-resort hotel located six minutes from the heart of the city. Impressive view over lake and mountains. Adjacent to its own, and only, golf course within Zurich city limits. Modern facilities in traditional architecture (1899). Also ideal for banquets, business and social activities. Dining – La Rotonde, one of Europe's top restaurants, with French cuisine and unique wine selection. Candlelight dinner with soft music every Wednesday. Barstubli and Garden Terrace for informal snacks and light meals.

Its entry left Nicholas in no doubt that here was a hotel he should visit for its setting, its number of rooms, its fine restaurants and its undoubted luxury status. The description settled it, although he was sceptical about the idea of a new Templar Order.

The seminar would be in the Easter vacation so he would be free to go. He sat down and immediately wrote a letter of acceptance.

Further consideration was interrupted with the door opening and the bright figure of Charlotte Fox-Travers appearing. She looked a picture of health, her cheeks rosy from cycling in the cold and her brown eyes smiling and sparkling. She had brown hair, neatly cut and shaped so that it framed her face, topped with a fringe. She took off her coat to reveal that she was wearing a white polo-neck sweater over a tweed skirt. A wide brown leather belt emphasised the slimness of her waist and her sweater flattered the beauty of her breasts, which Nicholas had to admit haunted him in his sleeping hours.

'Sorry to barge in on you Nicholas, but I had to see you.

I realise you're probably cataloguing your Valentines from your student fans, but I have just received an astonishing invitation to attend a symposium in Zurich in the Easter vacation and I want your opinion.'

'Snap,' replied Nicholas as he went over to her to take her coat and give her a kiss. He pointed to his invitation on the mantelpiece. 'Will you have one of my excellent coffee chocolate mixtures?'

She nodded her head. 'What a hoot – you being invited as well!'

They sat by the fire, Nicholas in his chair and Charlotte on a cushion by his feet. She had taken a sheaf of paper from her bag and handed it to him.

'I found all this off the net and printed some of it. You can have a good read through but basically they call themselves Knights Templars and claim to be true descendants of the original. They apparently speak of a hidden community which existed after the fall of the Templars in the fourteenth century and have now come back to the world announcing that they are dedicated to works of international charity, particularly to create secure accommodation for pilgrims in the Holy Land and with a mission to get the Temple Mount in Jerusalem administered by the United Nations. They seem already to have some presence in the United Nations carrying out work amongst refugees in the Middle East.'

Nicholas looked pensive. 'Claiming to be descended from some hidden line of Templar Knights sounds unbelievable. I realise I must have been invited because of my worldwide reputation as a Templar scholar, but why you?'

Charlotte snorted, 'Well you've obviously forgotten my authoritative paper on "The Shroud" in *History Today,* in which I covered the possibility of it being possessed by the original Templars. You may also remember my subsequent appearance on that BBC2 programme.'

Nicholas ignored this. 'It's interesting that such

specialised studies should have been spotted by our hosts to be. What's the point of asking us? Are they wanting us to give respectability to their claims, or are they wanting some further knowledge that they think we possess?'

Charlotte replied, 'I tried to get some information about them from their website. What it reveals is pretty bland. They evidently have a Grand Master based in a so-called Temple of Jerusalem in an old Templar castle near Zurzach, Switzerland, a town on the Swiss–German border. They also have twelve so-called Masters responsible for their houses in North and South America, Scandinavia and the United Kingdom. Further afield they have houses in Australia, India and Japan. Each one of them seems to own property, so they must be loaded.'

Their discussion was interrupted by the telephone ringing. Nicholas picked it up.

'Hi, Theo – ' a long pause – 'you're in Glastonbury! How is your book on the Grail progressing? The subject is hot now, isn't it? That absurd *Da Vinci Code* book engaging excessive publicity.' There was a further long pause while Nicholas listened to the American caller. Charlotte got up and studied the books on his shelves while Nicholas kept saying, 'Aha' and 'Yep' at regular intervals until moving into conversational mode again with a yelp of pleasure. 'Oh, Theo, that's great! I'm going to be in Zurich too, and my friend Charlotte – you remember her – you met her at that party in London and she joined our jam session afterwards, playing her violin. Yes, yes, I know she's very pretty and I'm repeating what you say because she is with me here ... ' Further conversation continued from the Greek–American, until Nicholas said, 'OK, that sounds good, we'll meet for lunch in Zurich before going to the seminar. Look forward to that. Cheers, Theo.'

He turned to Charlotte. 'As you've probably gathered, Theo Popadopoulos is going to be at the seminar. By the way, he wished you a happy Valentine's Day. So, that adds a Grail expert to their guest list.'

Charlotte clapped her hands. 'If he's going to be there, that decides it for me. Lovely hunk of a man and a dreamy trumpeter.' Nicholas put on a hurt expression. Charlotte, in a North Country accent, said, 'Don't take on, luv,' moved over to him and kissed him. 'By the way, I got you a Valentine present.' She handed him an envelope. 'It's a Gilbert and Sullivan disc including that chorus you like so much from *Iolanthe* – the entry of the lords singing, "Bow down, ye lower-middle classes." I thought it appropriate in view of your jealousy of my upper-class background.'

They both burst out laughing, their relationship at this stage of courtship was of continuous joshing, a camouflage for the growing realisation that they were falling seriously in love with each other.

Nicholas put on the disc. As the chorus sang, 'Bow down, ye lower-middle classes', the door burst open and his next-door neighbour entered, one Fred Clegg. His face was contorted with fury. He was a postgraduate student doing a doctorate in Information Technology. Two nights before, he had stood next to Nicholas in the college bar and drunkenly accused him of being a public-school snob and a dilettante historian, while *he* was at work on matters too complicated for Nicholas to grasp.

'I'm doing a man's work and proud of my lower-middle class origins,' he had said, but now he was standing in the doorway his conversation was more succinct. 'You toffee-nosed bugger ... ' and then seeing the astonished Charlotte, 'I'm not apologising. I didn't realise you had company, but if you play that fascist crap again, I'll thump you.' He left the room, slamming the door.

Nicholas burst out laughing and touched a switch to play the chorus again. 'We hit an unexpected target.'

Their mutual enjoyment of Gilbert and Sullivan was again

interrupted by a telephone call from the College Chaplain. He was in a state of high excitement.

'Nick, I need your support urgently, can you come over? The Master's bullying me again.'

Nicholas put his hand over the mouthpiece, raised his eyebrows and whispered, 'Father Francis is in a tizzy again, I'm afraid I'll have to go.' Charlotte smiled and nodded. Nicholas removed his hand. 'Of course, Francis, give me a few minutes.'

Charlotte put on her coat and came over and kissed him on both cheeks. 'See you tonight. Remember we are rehearsing in the New Court at Clare.'

They had recently been asked to join a new orchestra, Saint Cecilia's, which was attracting an enthusiastic following. Apart from the challenge to Nicholas's clarinet skills, he found Charlotte's absorption in her violin playing a delight to behold; he had had a great-uncle who had confided to him that he found that the greatest pleasure in attending concerts was that he could watch women play – perhaps it was hereditary.

When he entered the Chaplain's room, Nicholas found Father Francis standing at his window. He was lucky to have rooms looking over the River Cam to the lawns beyond. On one side of these, tall trees were casting shadows and the ground was still sparkling white with frost. Father Francis turned to greet him and beckoned him to join him at the window.

'I try to get strength from this view and from living the perfect Athenian good life, but it's all mucked up by our Master, the pompous ass, Canon Frobisher. My ancient College remit is total responsibility for the College Chapel, but he keeps sticking his oar in.'

Nicholas and Francis had been at school together at Melbury College, a joint foundation with Michaelhouse. The only drawback of their friendship was that Nicholas continually had to support the Chaplain in his battles with the Master.

Francis continued, 'The Master is telling me to act like a spokesman for the Government and is ordering me that in my sermons I have to warn students about a new Templar cult recruiting in the University. I mean, why can't he send a note round to everybody – I've got better things to do.'

'Crikey,' exclaimed Nicholas. 'Do you know anything about this movement?'

Francis sighed. 'No, I didn't really take that much in and know no more than something about them having their HQ in Switzerland and spreading worldwide. Evidently the authorities fear they might be a rebirth of that Order of the Solar Temple; you may remember that it became a suicide cult and was accused of stabbing babies with wooden stakes, though ridiculously attracting a good number of rich and famous people, people rumoured to include Princess Grace of Monaco.'

'How very interesting,' said Nicholas, who afterwards concluded that this was a massive understatement on his part.

Francis was more concerned with his own troubles and continued to complain. 'I mean, when will this interference stop? Next I will be told to sermonise against the consumption of gaseous foods to aid the fight against global warming!' Francis laughed at his own jest, but Nicholas was disconcerted by this news about the Templars and took his leave.

3

Three weeks later Nicholas, Charlotte and the American, Theo, arrived in Zurich. They had all collected further information about their hosts and had been sent the programme for the seminar. They had agreed to meet for lunch at the Kronenhall, a famous restaurant in Zurich, before proceeding to the hotel, where a reception for delegates was scheduled for six o'clock that evening.

The restaurant was full and buzzing with animated customers enjoying its warmth and good food, while outside it was snowing in a last blast of winter. Theo had reserved a table and was already there when Nicholas and Charlotte arrived from the airport. They agreed to order drinks and lunch before comparing notes.

Theo was able to give details of their hosts. It appeared that a Father Solomon, claiming to be an Armenian priest, had arrived in America three years ago, where there was a sizeable diaspora of Armenian Christians, and he began to preach a crusade to recover control of Jerusalem from Israel and to make it a UN protectorate. He claimed to have spent time at a monastery in Asia Minor where the Holy Grail of the Templars survived and where the guru Gondrieff had claimed to have learned his occult mysteries early in the twentieth century, before founding – in Moscow in 1912 – his institute for the Harmonious Development of Man. This monastery was called the Sarmouz.

Nicholas had been able to tell them more about Gondrieff. He told them that a well-known mystic called Ouspensky had met Gondrieff in 1915 and had become a disciple and a cult had developed. Gondrieff displayed all the symptoms of a cult leader with an overpowering, charismatic personality, claiming he could lead his followers to a higher level of consciousness. His disciple, Ouspensky, created a circle of influential people interested in these theories, including T. S. Eliot, Katherine Mansfield and Herbert Read. The third wife of the architect Frank Lloyd Wright was also an enthusiastic disciple.

Gondrieff never identified the exact locality of this spiritual centre, the Sarmouz. Its members wished to be undisturbed and guarded secret spiritual knowledge. This contemporary charismatic leader was preaching not only a crusade but also, like Gondrieff, hinting at knowledge of higher spiritual power. What was original was his claim that at the mysterious Sarmouz there remained a community of contemplative Templars, sworn to secrecy and avoiding outside contact. When the original Order had been destroyed at the beginning of the fourteenth century by the French King Philip IV, there had been left a small community of Templars in Asia Minor who had fled there by sea from their famous Middle Eastern castle at Acre when besieged by Suleiman. They took with them not only holy treasures, but also the secret occult knowledge rumoured to be possessed by the Templars. After the destruction of their Order, they had remained hidden, but had continued from the fourteenth century until the present day with a belief that one day their Order would be revived by a holy leader, who would save again the Holy Land for Christians. These descendants of the Templar Order had elected the new Grand Master, saying they all had simultaneous visions and dreams that he was to be the holy leader. He had left them to revive the Order.

Theo had seen him interviewed on American television and confirmed that he was definitely a charismatic leader: tall, in his mid-thirties, with long dark hair and a beard. His appearance was modelled on some of the modern stereotype images of Christ. He had interviewed well and had a deep voice and measured way of speaking. He had obviously hit the jackpot in tapping into a movement of fundamentalists strong in America, whose ambition was to recover the Temple Mount in Jerusalem and destroy the Muslim mosque there – the third most holy site of Islam.

On another level, there is a wide range of Christians who feel the whole of the Holy Land should be made safe for pilgrims and that control of it under some United Nations organisation would be preferable to the current horrors of the Israeli and Palestinian struggle. This resurrection of the Templar Order was a romantic manifestation of a broader desire for stability in the Middle East.

Theo had said that the Grand Master had been evasive when asked to prove the existence of this hidden community of Templars and to speak of his election as holy leader, saying he had sworn to keep its whereabouts secret.

At this point Nicholas had been unable to control his scepticism. He pointed out that however remote this community of so-called Templars was, it was unlikely its story would have remained hidden for seven hundred years. What surprised him was its phenomenal growth. Nicholas could only assume these members were attracted by the desire to belong to a growing romantic organisation. He had seen pictures of their gatherings with groups of men dressed as Hollywood-type Templars. It could be an enormous confidence trick. He told them both about the warning the University had received.

At this statement Charlotte had nodded in agreement. 'What worries me is what part are we meant to play? I understand that the lecturers have dubious academic backgrounds, from what Nicholas has told me, with doctorates from obscure small American universities. My intuition is that we have been asked to give the proceedings intellectual respectability. I see we are listed as attending along with other well-known historians. Let's face it, we're here because of the lush attractions of the location. Can we agree on the real facts as we know them?'

The two men nodded in agreement.

Theo said, 'I've just read that brilliant satire, *Foucault's Pendulum*. In it one of the characters was asked how one would recognise a lunatic; the answer was that "sooner or later they talk about the Templars".' He let out one of his unique yelps of laughter so that they all joined in until Nicholas said, 'I suggest that we précis what the proven facts are and Charlotte should write them down when we get to the hotel.'

Charlotte laughed. 'Hardly a fair division of labour, but my note-taking at lectures is renowned – I'll do my best.'

While they exchanged information they were able to enjoy a delicious meal, and Charlotte's note-taking was finished by the time coffee arrived. Afterwards they collected their luggage from the restaurant cloakroom and proceeded by taxi to the Dolder Grand Hotel.

They were immediately engulfed by a welcoming committee of the Templars, men and women dressed in mock-silver mesh material, over which they wore white tabards with large red Templar crosses emblazoned on the front and back. They gave their names and were immediately assigned rooms and their luggage whisked away, to arrive there almost at the same time as they were guided to them by the hotel staff. It was all very efficient. In each of their rooms was a clear timetable of the events of the weekend, summaries of the lecture subjects and a potted biography of each speaker. Nicholas revelled in the understated luxury of his room, and the feeling that he was staying in a hotel in which generations of guests had enjoyed great comfort and efficient service.

4

At eight the next morning Nicholas was sitting in the Dolder Grand at a table in his room, wrapped in a fluffy bathrobe and eating a full English breakfast with coffee and orange juice, and watching BBC World on television.

Theo was in a tracksuit and tucking into a plate of ham and eggs accompanied by muffins, and watching CNN.

Charlotte was in a dark blue, silk robe, watching the stock market report on the Bloomfield channel. She was drinking peppermint tea and limiting herself to a grapefruit. Secretly she exercised daily in a struggle to keep trim.

A Colonel from MI6-66, Baker by name, had arrived the night before on the last flight from London and was in his room in the Holiday Inn near Kloten airport watching Swiss television news. It featured the arrival from America the day before of the Grand Master of the revived Templar Order. He was a tall figure in an Armenian priest's black cloak with a hood covering the top of his face, but a close-up showed a young man with long black hair, well groomed like a woman's and a hint of very blue eyes: could they be tinted lenses, wondered the Colonel? Two smaller figures, similarly cloaked, walked on either side of him like minders. Cameras flashed as he was filmed getting into a large Mercedes Maybach limousine. He turned before getting in the car and made a large sign of the cross over the photographers and puzzled travellers coming out of the airport building. The TV commentator told the viewers that this was the Master of the controversial Templar Order, returning from a visit to the States and en route to the Templar Castle at Zurzack, reminding them that it was claimed he had prophesied the 9/11 disaster six months before it occurred.

'Very interesting,' the Colonel murmured out loud as he spread a spoon of honey over his toast and sipped at a large espresso coffee. He wrote a brief note in a black loose-leaf folder and ordered a taxi to take him to the Dolder Grand. On arrival he checked in at a desk outside the conference room. In return he received a programme and a list of delegates. He was given a plastic badge indicating he was Colonel Baker, Military Historian. He found a milling throng making its way into the room; he reckoned there must be over a hundred people there already, all talking loudly to each other.

At ten o'clock two men came on to the platform at the far end of the room. They were both dressed in the uniform of the Templars. One of them rang a sonorous bell and put up his hand for silence. He introduced himself as the Chairman. He was a tall, young blond with a matching beard. He began by welcoming all present and explained that he was Master of the Swiss and German Templars. He said they were starting proceedings at that time as it had allowed delegates to fly in overnight from the Americas and the Far East. He explained that the time for each lecture would be forty minutes with twenty minutes for questions. The end of the lecture he signalled by the ringing of the bell, a bell he said was a gift to their Grand Master from the hidden monastery of Sarmouz, where – as some of them knew – the Holy Grail was kept in safety. There was a murmur of interest from the audience, but disrupted by a snort of derision from a large fat man sitting in the front row.

The speaker hesitated, glared at the man and continued, 'This bell has been blessed by water from the Grail and therefore is itself sacred and I hope you will honour it.'

Nicholas, Theo and Charlotte were seated together in the middle of the room. They exchanged glances and Nicholas whispered, 'I hope we are going to rise intellectually above this sort of hocus pocus.'

The Chairman turned to his fellow Templar.

'It is now my great honour to introduce our first speaker, our Templar Knight Sebastian, who is also our Guest Master at the Temple of Zurzack. He is going to give you an outline of the New Templar Order and its organisation today. He will also run through the programme of the seminar.'

Sebastian was short and rotund, reflecting his enthusiastic participation in providing generous hospitality. He sported a goatee beard, at which he tugged between sentences.

'You should all have a programme of today's seminar', he began. 'Meals will be in the main hotel dining room and drinks of all types will be available in the foyer. You are also welcome to use the hotel's comfortable lounges and bar: all orders are with the compliments of the Order.' Here there was a murmur of appreciation, especially from borderline alcoholics. He went on to explain that there would be continuous transport to the airport when the final lecture finished at tea time. He then went on to outline the history of the Templars.

Frankly it was a boring lecture, rather mechanically delivered, and it seemed to last longer than its allotted forty minutes. Muted applause greeted its end along with a few murmured alleluias from Templars in the audience.

The Templar Chairman of the meeting stood up and announced that it was time for questions and discussion; microphones would be brought to those who would like to speak if they would first raise their hands. The fat man at the front, who had snorted loudly at the beginning when the Grail was mentioned, put up his hand along with four others among the rest of the audience. He was ignored and an old woman in a red dress was given a microphone. She asked a long question about the compliance of the Pope in allowing Philip IV of France to smash the Order in the fourteenth century. She went on to answer her own question at length by giving a mini-lecture. Eventually the Chairman said thank you.

He then nodded to a man sitting in the second row who asked what was known about the Templar fleet that got away from La Rochelle before being seized by the forces of the King and reputedly taking the Templar treasures with them to an unknown destination. Could those treasures not have been the Grail and the Shroud of Turin?

A buzz of interest rose from the audience; most of them knew well the history of the end of the Templars but this was the meat they had come to dissect.

The Chairman frowned. 'You will have seen that these matters are specifically mentioned in the programme for this afternoon's lecture. I think we should leave discussion of these matters until then.'

This announcement produced a further snort from the fat man in the front row, who suddenly got up and walked along until opposite the questioner holding the microphone in the second row.

Nicholas whispered to Charlotte, 'That's that Welsh mad-man, Professor Darren Jones from Jesus College, Oxford; thinks he's a leading expert on the Holy Grail.'

The Professor snatched at the microphone.

The holder shouted, 'Hang on, I haven't finished.'

A struggle developed and a noise of general disapproval arose, though there was some laughter as well.

The Chairman shouted, 'Sit down that man.'

Professor Darren Jones might have been big and fat but he was strong and he wrenched the microphone away into his own hand. A hush fell as his voice boomed out, drowning the order repeated by the Chairman to sit down.

'I want to make a statement and I prefer to make it standing. I hope our time here is not going to be wasted by fairy tales about the Holy Grail. My book, to be pub-lished in July, will prove conclusively that the Grail was at

Glastonbury Abbey in England. After the dissolution of that monastery it was taken safely to Wales to a faithful family called Powell, living in Nanteous House, where the Prior of Glastonbury became their Chaplain. This is the true Grail and is presently in a bank vault in Herefordshire, England.'

During this outburst, the Chairman had nodded to two Templars sitting at the end of the fourth row. They stood up and strode powerfully towards the Professor, who was oblivious of them as they came up behind him. Immediately his voice was lost as one of the advancing Templars took hold of the microphone. Professor Darren Jones was strong but it was removed from him as if it were a rattle from a feeble baby. Then each of the Templars pinned the Professor's elbows to his side and marched him back to his chair.

The Chairman put up his hand. 'A most unseemly interruption. I think we should now finish and proceed to drinks before lunch.'

There was a short burst of applause and after the Chairman had left the platform, an outburst of excited chatter and laughter. This was not shared by Colonel Baker, who looked pensive.

Colonel Baker had placed himself on the front row so that he could enjoy a close view of the speakers. When the Chairman of the meeting had come on to the platform, Colonel Baker had to rub his eyes and clean the monocle that he carried in the top pocket of his blazer. The Chairman was the spitting image of a young, military historian who had taught him at Sandhurst thirty years before, save that he now had a blond beard matching his long hair, instead of the clipped military moustache that had been sported by the Sandhurst doppelgänger. It was obviously his son or nephew, but it left the Colonel disturbed. He had been amazed to see a scar on the left side of the Chairman's face reddening, exactly as happened with his Sandhurst double when he was angry all those years ago. He sat in his seat, lost in thought, and then picked up the list of delegates and studied it before getting up and joining a throng outside the dining room enjoying drinks before going inside to attack tables groaning with lavish plates of buffet food.

The Welsh Professor, Darren Jones, was being consoled by three Indian delegates. Colonel Baker worked his way through the crowd, his keen eyesight taking in everyone's name badge. He spotted his prey and joined Nicholas, who was with Theo and Charlotte.

'Excuse me joining you.' He introduced himself and later joined them at a table for the buffet lunch.

'Have you come for the hotel, the food and the booze, like most of us?' asked Theo.

The Colonel looked demure. 'Not really. I lecture on the Crusades sometimes at Sandhurst and thought I might glean some up-to-date information here.' Later he had turned to Nicholas. 'Could you spare me a moment when we go out of here for the coffee break?'

When they both had coffee in their hands, the Colonel lowered his voice. 'I wonder if we could have a private word and carry on upstairs in your room?'

Nicholas found himself replying, 'Yes, of course, but "carrying on upstairs in my room" sounds a flirtatious invitation.'

The Colonel frowned. 'Perhaps you would like to lead the way ... '

When they entered Nicholas's room, the Colonel put his forefinger to his lips and whispered, 'Don't speak.' He produced a silver torch-like object and went over to the phone and then waved it over some of the pictures and disappeared into the bathroom. Nicholas stood amazed as he heard the sound of the bathwater being run. The Colonel reappeared and turned on the television at high volume and went back into the bathroom, beckoning Nicholas to follow. Nicholas joined him in the bathroom, now full of steam, and was unable to stop fantasising that he would suddenly see the Colonel stripping off his clothes. In fact the Colonel opened the window a little and cold air rushed in, clearing the fog: it had begun to snow outside.

Colonel Baker sat on the edge of the bath and motioned to Nicholas to sit on a towel-padded stool next to him. He leaned forward and said in low voice, 'Your bedroom is bugged – probably they all are. We don't have much time until the lectures start again at two o'clock. Here's my card.'

Nicholas looked at the card. It said Colonel Baker OBE, Military Historian, Sandhurst. The Colonel took it and wrote quickly on the back 'MI6 Section 66 (Cults)' and two telephone numbers. He turned on the bath taps more fully and again they were enveloped in steam. The television could be heard delivering the news in Swiss German.

'Listen carefully. MI6 has a little-known department 66 which was set up to monitor and name dangerous cults which move in on the young in a big way. A few years ago there were dotty Indian gurus, Red Brigades and a nasty American import – the Process, a satanic cult – all that type of thing. Now we are heavily involved in monitoring Islamic extremists. This does not exclude us from our original intent and this Templar lot are worrying. They are recruiting in the top universities. I should like to meet you in England and tell you more. At the same time, I need your help.'

Nicholas nodded. 'Of course.'

The Colonel went on. 'Right, I would like a résumé of the rest of your time here. I gather you have been asked to the symposium afterwards which the Grand Master is attending. These seminars have been held before, in America recently, and in India and Japan. They were also followed by these smaller symposiums and a few attending them have been asked to do research for them in their castle at Zurzach. The results seem to have been unfortunate; we have reports from families and universities hinting at some sort of brain-washing and some of them get sucked into this Templar organisation. This is bad news, as we have reason to suspect that the organisation is a cover for something frighteningly dangerous. I'll explain when we meet again in England. So, if you get an invitation at the symposium to do research with them, please accept it. We shall give you psychological briefing and protection if you do.'

Nicholas looked surprised. 'Already this lot seem pretty ridiculous to me – a bit of a hoot.'

The Colonel put a firm hand on Nicholas's knee and looked him straight in the eye. 'Don't make light of it, this is no hoot, I can assure you. The first telephone number I gave you is manned twenty-four hours a day at our Whitehall office, the second is my mobile number – an especially power-ful model for accredited intelligence services. Don't hesitate to contact me at any time. When you get through say, "Cat's-Eyes"; that's me. When contact is made then say, "Twenty-four eggs." You're going to be our man "Twenty-Four" on this trail and "eggs" means we scramble whatever phone you are calling from. Got it?'

Nicholas stood up and saluted. 'For Queen and country – sah.'

The Colonel suppressed a smile. 'OK. Repeat my instructions.'

Nicholas did as requested.

The Colonel stood up. 'OK, we'll meet in London. Ring me as soon as you're back. You'll have to go through the formality of signing the Official Secrets Act before I tell you more.'

Nicholas interrupted. 'I have two close friends here also going to the symposium. I can absolutely trust them. May I include them, provided they swear to sign the Official Secrets Act when we meet in London?' Nicholas gave the Colonel a brief description of Charlotte and Theo.

The Colonel stood silently for a moment and then said, 'OK, but tell them that we regard the whole matter as extremely dangerous.' As he left, the Colonel nodded towards the booming television. 'I'll leave you to catch up with the Swiss weather forecast – sounds as if we've got snow coming.'

When he had gone, Nicholas turned off the television and went to the window. As he looked up, large snowflakes were falling lazily towards him before drifting slowly down to add to the white blanket thickening below.

5

When Nicholas returned downstairs, the delegates were moving into the Conference Room for the afternoon lecture. As he joined the queue, he found himself next to three Indians who smiled warmly at him and shook his hand, rattling off their names. Nicholas asked where they came from and they answered, laughing, 'Kerala, India. We are St Thomas's Christians.' Nicholas remembered the Nestorian Churches of Kerala, said to have been founded by the Apostle St Thomas.

He saw his friends in the same seats they had occupied in the morning and went to join them. Nicholas noted that the Colonel was back again at the front of the room, looking pensively at the programme.

As Nicholas sat down, his hand was shaken by an Arab dressed in a flowing white robe. He introduced himself to Nicholas as Professor Mahoud from Jerusalem, and whispered, 'I'm here as an observer. The Templars have just opened a hospital near my mosque in Jerusalem and I'm trying to find out more about them. Can we meet later?' He gave Nicholas his card and later on he was to have a discussion with Theo which was to prove invaluable. Further conversation was interrupted as the Templar Chairman of the morning session entered the room, followed by a bald-headed man whose face was framed by a large, white beard. He was wearing an over-large brown tweed jacket, covering a plum-coloured polo-neck sweater, with beige jeans and white shoes. The Chairman rang his bell and introduced the speaker.

'Professor Berlinger, from Berkeley University, California. Professor Berlinger has a worldwide reputation for his great knowledge of the Templars, about whom he has published two very successful books. He is going to tell us today the truth about a subject of great interest to us all: the Holy Treasures of the Templars.'

The Professor shambled to the front of the platform, placed his notes on a stand and adjusted the microphone. There was loud applause. He blew his nose and turned to the microphone.

'It's a great pleasure to be here in Zurich again and to be amongst my impressive Templar friends whose work we all admire. Firstly, the Chairman has asked me to say that during questions at the end, anyone speaking out of turn or for too long will have his microphone switched off.'

There was a ripple of applause at this point. The lecturer spoke well, in a melodious voice. He peppered his lecture with amusing asides, and although Nicholas was sceptical, he produced a coherent history of the Templar claims to having possessed the Holy Grail and the Shroud of Turin for part of their history. He described how the first Templars, who were few in number, arrived in Jerusalem and started excavations under the Temple of Solomon. Here they found the Holy Grail and, he said in a pointed aside, 'This was a real vessel, not the esoteric nonsense concerning Mary Magdalene marrying Christ and producing a child, plus all that Merovingian rot of royal descendants as used as a theme by pulp American writers.'

He went on to say that after this discovery of the Grail, the Templar numbers and influence expanded exponentially. Because of their probity, they became bankers for the medieval world, building their castles in the Middle East and through Europe, where their wealth was well protected. They were able to buy the Shroud of Turin, and certainly its image was used in Templar worship: its likeness could be found in Templar houses throughout the Order. He cited a recent discovery in Temple Combe, Somerset, England, of a ceiling revealing this image in a thirteenth-century room.

Sadly the Shroud had to be sold to support the remnants of the Templar Order after its cruel suppression, no doubt some of the proceeds going to the hidden Templars in the Sarmouz monastery, where they had taken the Holy Grail.

He continued by saying, 'Unfortunately the whereabouts of the Grail today is more problematic. You have already heard this is a secret location in Asia Minor, closely guarded. Because of its spiritual power its location must remain secret, otherwise it would be in constant danger of abduction. Only the community at Sarmouz and the twelve territorial Masters of the revived Templar Order have seen it and can testify to its power, part of which has enabled the Grand Master to have the gift of prophecy. As you know, this is a gift he uses sparingly.'

There were scattered cries of 'Alleluia,' from the Templars in the room.

The irrepressible Darren Jones stood up again and shouted, 'This is all arrant nonsense, the speaker is a brain-washed supernumerary of the Templar Order; this Grail is a fraud to con you all. I can prove it!'

The two Templars, who had manhandled him before lunch, leapt to their feet and ran to pinion him by the elbows again and drag the Professor out of the room. He resisted, shouting, 'Let go, you louts,' and to the astonished audience, 'You'll find the truth in my book, *The True Grail*, to be published this summer ... '

The Templar bouncers re-doubled their efforts and lifted him off the floor so that he looked as if he was on an imaginary bicycle as his legs pedalled in mid-air. Still shouting, he was thrown through the swing doors and stumbled out into the area beyond. The two Templars followed and a faint cry was heard, and then silence.

The Chairman rang his bell to quell the volume of protest coming from the audience; Colonel Baker noticed the scar on his face reddening.

'Please remain seated, we cannot tolerate such abuse of a distinguished lecturer, nor have our true message distorted. Please continue, Professor Berlinger.'

After this disturbance the Professor brought his lecture to an abrupt end and the ensuing question time was subdued. The meeting broke up and the delegates were told that there would be an hour's free time before tea and excellent Swiss chocolate cake. Except for those staying for the symposium, the seminar was over and most would be leaving in an organised rota of buses to the airport or station at Kloten, Zurich.

Colonel Baker collected his coat from the hotel cloakroom and decided he needed some fresh air before leaving for the airport. The snow had stopped and the long drive from the hotel had already been cleared, which enabled him to take a walk. It was nearly dark when he reached the hotel on his return. There was a mini-bus parked outside the entrance and the three Indian delegates were standing beside it, stamping their feet and engaged in animated conversation. They stopped talking as the Colonel approached and saluted him.

'Most unfortunate we have to leave for London tonight – you too perhaps? We await the naughty Professor man and his luggage.'

The Colonel replied, 'Have a good journey. An unfortunate ending for the Welshman.'

The Indians giggled, 'Very unfortunate end.'

Colonel Baker waved at them and went inside to see a very pale Professor Jones being escorted outside with his luggage. He was warmly greeted by the Indians.

'Come on then, we shall have a good party at the airport – drinks on us!'

The mini-bus moved sedately down the drive and set off in the darkness through the woods behind the hotel. The Professor did not remember these trees when he arrived, but he was too weak and shaken to make any remark. After he had been thrown through the doors of the Conference Room, the two Templars had taken him into the lift and beaten him up and then, arriving on his floor, dragged him to his room. Passing an amazed maid on the way, they had shaken their heads, 'Drunken British.' They got the maid to open the door of his room, and put him on his bed.

The mini-bus with the Professor and the Indians on board was travelling slowly, as the road was icy. The driver's telephone gave a shrill ring and a long conversation ensued. He turned the vehicle into a lay-by and announced, 'I'm afraid your London plane has been cancelled due to bad weather at Heathrow. However, the Templar Guest Master suggests you stay overnight at their headquarters in Zurzach. He says it is warm and very comfortable.'

The Indians broke out into excited cries of delight. This news made the Professor feel more distressed, however. He thought to himself, that if he felt strong enough he would get out when the mini-bus stopped at the next traffic lights. One of the Indians tapped him on the shoulder. 'This is going to be a better party than the one planned for the airport!'

The Professor's short reply was, 'Ouch.' He felt as if his shoulder had been stung by a wasp, then he slumped sideways against the Indian, who giggled, 'Dear, dear, so tired after his exciting day,' as he put the spent syringe into a plastic box in his briefcase.

Half an hour later they drove through the entrance to the ancient Templar Castle in Zurzach. As they entered the courtyard, a portcullis dropped behind them and cut off the rest of the world. It was snowing again.

Two Templars came down some steps carrying a stretcher. They were closely followed by a red-haired woman, of late middle age and strongly built. She walked round the minibus and opened the driver's door. At the same time the stretcher bearers heaved the unconscious Professor out and carried him off into the castle.

Meanwhile, in the Dolder Grand, Colonel Baker was waiting to have a quick word with Nicholas after the last lecture. 'Can you step outside for a moment? It's finished snowing.' Nicholas followed him out. The Colonel produced from his side pocket a small package. 'I have a curious request: this packet contains a bottle of 4711 Eau de Cologne.' Nicholas began to wonder again about the Colonel's intentions. The Colonel continued, 'I'd rather you told your friends the information I gave you when you are safely away from being overheard, but I want the help of the three of you in a small genetic experiment.'

At this moment the wind blew a lump of snow off a window-sill above them. It whooshed between them and hit the ground with a thump, obscuring the Colonel's last sentence, which Nicholas thought had ended with ' ... a small genital experiment ... ' and rather abruptly replied, 'What the hell are you talking about now – a genital experiment?'

For a moment the Colonel lost his cool demeanour. 'No, no, *genetic* experiment. Don't get alarmed, I'll explain. When I was at Sandhurst, I was lectured by a double of the Chairman who started the proceedings this morning. This double was allergic to 4711 Cologne, and it triggered in him serious asthmatic attacks. Some of the crueller members of the College cottoned on to this and deliberately doused themselves with it so that his lectures had to be cancelled and they could take time off for more leisurely pursuits. In the end, we were forbidden to wear it when he came to lecture. He was based at the Imperial War Museum, and his name was Major Franks. Now this was over thirty years ago, so this chap here must be his son or nephew.

'After lunch I approached him and said quietly, "Major Franks?" He didn't look at me but absolutely froze and stopped talking to the person with him and began to cough

36

uncontrollably. When he had recovered I said, "Sorry to interrupt you, but are you the son of a Crusader expert called Major Franks, whom I knew at Sandhurst many years ago?" He took a while to stop coughing. He then denied it, denied it with unnecessary vehemence, I thought, saying he was a Templar Knight by the name of Master Karl and had lived in Zurzach for many years. All very odd, but I got my secretary to check at lunchtime with the Imperial War Museum. They said Major Franks had left them twenty-five years ago to go to the Porton Down Research Establishment, and had published some scientific papers on nutrition and drugs to be used by astronauts if they should try and travel beyond the moon. We didn't know he had any scientific qualifications, so I suppose the Crusades were just a hobby. Anyway, my genetic experiment is this – did his aversion to 4711 pass genetically to a son or relation? I should like you to take this bottle of 4711 and, with your friends, wear it and gather round him at the symposium this evening. It's all very rum – you know this Master Karl even has exactly the same voice as his Sandhurst look-alike.'

Nicholas brushed some of the fallen snow off his arm.

'Well, talking of rum, you've introduced a rum dimension into our lives, so in for a penny, in for a pound. I'll try and get my friends to help, unless in Switzerland one can be sectioned for insane behaviour.'

The Colonel slapped him on the back. 'Good man! I'll see you and your friends in London.'

Nicholas bade farewell to the Colonel and went to find his friends Theo and Charlotte. He asked them to get their coats and join him for a walk so that they could have a breath of bracing air before changing for the symposium. The invitation had indicated a black-tie event.

Charlotte shook her head. 'I must wash my hair before this party tonight.'

Nicholas took her arm and whispered, 'If you love me,

please come – I've got vital news you need to know about our host.'

Her eyes widened. 'OK, but don't take my acceptance as a declaration of love; that's a strong word, Nick!'

Theo had not heard this exchange, but immediately agreed and went off to get his coat. Ten minutes later they were gingerly walking down the drive of the hotel; the frost was making the road slippery even though it had been cleared of snow. As they walked either side of Nicholas, they listened to him with increasing amazement, but agreed to co-operate in the task the Colonel had set him. On balance it added piquancy to the event they were attending. Before they turned back, they felt it appropriate to shake hands.

'For Queen and country,' said Nicholas.

The snow began to fall again and covered their hair. As they walked back, the hotel appeared just a dull yellow glow at the top of the hill: a building that would reveal other surprises before the evening was finished.

6

The venue for the symposium was a room on the first floor of the hotel. At the entrance the guests had to enter under a detection frame similar to those used in airports. The two muscular Templars who had removed Professor Jones were there to check the partygoers entering the room. A lady Templar stood nearby, ticking off names and ready to search any females who set off the alarm.

When Nicholas eventually entered the room, he saw Charlotte was already there, drinking champagne with an exotically robed Armenian Bishop. He was wearing a black silk cape with an attached pointed hood covering his head. Nicholas joined them. Charlotte's eyes twinkled.

'Nicholas, this is Bishop Krasnos from Armenia.'

The Bishop inclined his head in solemn acknowledgement. Nicholas noticed that his black beard was wet with champagne: the Bishop was gulping it down, and extending his glass to have it refilled every time a waiter came near.

'The Bishop has visited Cambridge once,' said Charlotte. The Bishop bowed his head again but did not speak and instead took a loud slurp of champagne. Nicholas realised that he had come in on a one-sided conversation devoid of sparkling cocktail party repartee.

This turgid situation was interrupted by two men joining them, both wearing dinner jackets that appeared a little too small for their powerful frames. One of the men was standing behind the other in a deferential manner. The first one stepped in front of Charlotte, clicked his heels and bowed his head.

'My name is Sir Darcy de Malplaquet. I think you are all from England or America.' He turned to her companions. 'I am Master of the Templars in the UK.'

He shook their hands one by one except Charlotte's, which he raised to his lips.

Malplaquet, the English Master, was a tall man, over six foot three inches, so that his head was above those around him. His neck was thick and his black hair sleeked back with hair cream; his mouth was thin and topped by a black, pencil-thin moustache. He wore a red sash under his dinner jacket on which was attached the Templar seal, representing two men riding on a single horse. He looked very fit.

Nicholas studied him closely and instinctively felt uneasy. He concluded he was bogus with his kissing of hands and clipped manner of speaking. A silver-topped ebony cane completed the picture.

He told them they had just completed the restoration of a house in Temple Guiting in the Cotswolds, the site of an original Templar Preceptory. It was to be the headquarters of the Templar Order in the UK and he told them how delighted the Order was to have found this house in an old Templar village. They had found several artefacts including old tiling which had been incorporated during their restoration work.

He turned to his companion behind him and introduced him. 'This is Fred, one of our supernumeraries.'

Fred muttered ' 'Allo'. He was about five foot six, broad-shouldered and muscular. He could have been a bouncer in a nightclub.

Malplaquet said, 'Fred drives me about, that sort of thing, a bit of a treasure – what! Well now, let's take our seats. Here comes the Grand Master of the Order.'

They were rescued from further bombast by a small party entering the room whose arrival commanded everyone's attention. The small group were led by the Chairman of the day's event. He was followed by a striking-looking brunette in her early thirties. She was also wearing the Templar uniform, over which she wore a scarlet cape. Her dark hair was close cropped, which led Theo to say afterwards that she could audition for the part of Joan of Arc. The Grand Master of the Templar Order followed. He was wearing a white tuxedo over his black evening dress trousers and a white silk tabard with the Templar cross. He was even taller than Malplaquet, the British Templar. His dark hair was long and well groomed. He looked lean and fit and probably in his mid-thirties. His head was well proportioned and his black beard neatly trimmed. It was his eyes that were the most striking feature of his appearance; Charlotte was struck by their brilliant blue colour, sparkling like sapphires. He was bowing slightly to left and right as he moved forward and one felt he was absorbing the identity of each guest. Nicholas reckoned there must be at least forty people there with at least half having attended the seminar earlier.

At the front of the room there was a lectern faced by five lines of chairs. This left two-thirds of the room free and on one side there was a long buffet table groaning with dishes – plates containing large hams and turkeys and sides of beef. On one, a pig's head looked balefully at whole salmon and neatly arranged rows of lobsters. Small tables were scattered around the rest of the room.

The Grand Master's entourage sat down behind the lectern, facing the audience. The Chairman called for silence and the Grand Master came and stood beside him. The Chairman asked everyone to bring full glasses and find a seat, assuring them that the Grand Master would not keep them long from the excellent feast awaiting them. First he wished to say a few words of welcome and then take the opportunity of meeting them individually before they moved off to the buffet.

In a few moments everyone was seated and eager to hear what the Grand Master would say to them. They were not to be disappointed. He spoke slowly in English, with a slight American-Slavic accent; his voice was deep and mellow and what he said was emphasised by expressive movements of his hands. Nicholas noted with interest that he was wearing a large ring on which was imprinted the insignia of the Templar Order of two men riding on a single horse, ironically indicating the poverty of the original Order. Nicholas had managed to buy a similar one in a market in Istanbul when he had visited that city two years before.

The Grand Master welcomed them and thanked them for making time to come and visit Switzerland from many distant lands to attend their seminar, from which they would have learnt that the Templars were now established again worldwide. The Templars' historic calling was to secure the Holy Land for Christendom. It was not necessary for him to mention what danger threatened Jerusalem from the growing militancy of Islam. It was his urgent hope that circumstances would lead to the Holy City of Sion coming under the United Nations as soon as possible. At this point there was an outbreak of frenzied clapping and cheering, with cries of 'Amen' from the Templars present.

The Grand Master put up his hand for silence, and continued, 'I can do no better than conclude with the call to action that the great St Bernard gave us at the beginning of our Order.' His voice deepened before continuing with the historic words of the Saint.

'The Lord of Heaven is losing his land, the land in which he appeared to men, in which he lived amongst men for more than thirty years. You now have a cause for which you can fight without endangering your soul, a cause in which to win is glorious, and for which to die is but gain. Do not miss this opportunity. Take the sign of the cross. At once you will have indulgence for all the sins you confess with a contrite heart.'

This was greeted with further rapturous applause. The Chairman put up his hand and said that he would now be introducing them to the Grand Master before supper, and the evening would end with a solemn blessing. He requested that everyone move to the clear area of the room, where liquid refreshment would be available until the buffet opened.

Nicholas, Theo and Charlotte moved to the clear area of the room as requested. As they stood together the scent of 4711 Cologne was overwhelming; they had applied it liberally before arriving in the room so that Colonel Baker's genetic experiment could be carried out. They did not have to wait long. The Chairman approached them and began introducing them by name to the Grand Master, who cupped their proffered hands with both of his. Charlotte noticed his long fingers and thought what a splendid pianist he could be. Nicholas was able to study more closely the Grand Master's ring. It was exactly the same as his own and he decided he would raise it as a subject for discussion when the opportunity arose. The solemnity of these introductions was unexpectedly interrupted. The Chairman Karl, who had been standing in attendance, clutched his throat and staggered to a chair; his scarlet face contorted in the agony of apparently suffocation. His desperate attempts to draw breath were producing low whooping noises. One of the women accompanying the Grand Master rushed forward and produced from her bag a Ventolin inhaler.

The Grand Master moved over to stand solicitously by the choking man until the inhaler took effect; a nurse joined them and, after a short while, pronounced him sufficiently recovered to be assisted from the room. The Grand Master returned to Nicholas and apologised for leaving them and explained that Chairman Karl was an asthmatic and something must have triggered his attack. A young Templar approached with a silver tray on which were stiff white envelopes. The Grand Master looked at the names and carefully presented one each to Nicholas, Charlotte and Theo. A smaller envelope he gave to the Bishop, who was still standing by them. As he did so he said, 'We are engaged in a great task, a crusade that must be won. We believe you have knowledge that can help us in our work. It would please us if you could accept these invitations, which are asking you to come for six weeks at the beginning of your summer vacations. Our castle at Zurzach is historically very interesting and in our library you will find many books and documents of interest. You will be accommodated in a nearby hotel which has the advantage of an agreeable hot spring pool. During the day we shall look after you and feed you, but as we are a religious community our evenings are short as we observe "the Great Silence" after our evening service at seven o'clock.' As he handed an envelope to Charlotte, he said, 'Your expertise in the Shroud of Turin is of family importance to us and I'm sure you will find much of interest in our archives.' He turned to Nicholas. 'I think you also will find some documents which have not been properly studied concerning the remnants of the Templar Order after its suppression by the King of France. Finally, to your American brother here, I promise much material on the Holy Grail.'

He was about to address the Bishop when there came a penetrating cry from behind the serving table. A dark-complexioned man in a chef's hat had been noticed by Nicholas, assiduously carving a baron of beef; he had earmarked it for future consumption. Out of the corner of his eye, he saw this man throwing off his chef's hat and charging between the buffet tables towards their group, holding in front of him a long thin carving knife. He was moving fast like a cavalry man and screaming, 'Allah, Allah be praised.'

One of the Templars, who had been standing near them, leapt on the chef's back. This deflected the attacker from the Grand Master, but his momentum carried him forward even with the Templar on his back, and his knife sliced the flesh of the Bishop's wrist, severing an artery. The letter in the Bishop's hand fluttered to the ground, splattered with blood pouring from his wound.

Pandemonium broke out: the Bishop staggered to a chair, clutching his wrist with his other hand. Another Templar helped bring the assailant to the ground. The Grand Master and those near him backed away, knocking over some of the guests standing behind him. The room was hushed with shock. The attacker was dragged to his feet; the Grand Master picked up the knife and nodded. The silence was disturbed by the sound of a bone breaking as a Templar wrenched the arm of the chef behind his back – there was a terrible keening scream as he was removed.

Bedlam broke out with mingled screams and shouts. Charlotte thought she was going to faint and Nicholas thought he was going to be sick. The nurse appeared again through the crowd to help the Bishop by snatching a silk scarf from the neck of a nearby woman and using it to make a tourniquet around his arm.

The Grand Master put up his hand for silence. 'Our holy work brings us enemies, but God protects us. Unfortunately our evening has been spoilt by barbarity and some of you may now prefer to eat in your rooms or in the hotel dining room rather than here. Bow your heads while I give you our Templar blessing.' As soon as he finished, he beckoned to his entourage to join him and strode from the room holding the long carving knife lightly at his side.

'Cool, very cool,' said Theo. 'I suggest we go to my room for a strong drink.'

Nicholas nodded. 'I'll certainly go along with that.' He turned to take Charlotte's arm, but before doing so, bent down and picked up the bloodstained letter intended for the Bishop.

When they got to Theo's room the phone rang. It was Colonel Baker.

'Cat's-Eyes,' were his opening words.

Theo looked puzzled and handed the phone to Nicholas.

Colonel Baker repeated his *nom de guerre*.

'Twenty-four eggs,' replied Nicholas.

This charade relieved the tension and they all started to laugh.

Nicholas told Colonel Baker of the assassination attempt. To his surprise Colonel Baker replied, 'I know Al Qaeda is claiming responsibility. We need to meet in London as soon as possible; can you get back here by two-thirty tomorrow afternoon?'

Nicholas consulted the others and they nodded their agreement. Colonel Baker gave Nicholas his address at the War Office in Whitehall.

When he put the phone down, Theo said, 'This goes from the bizarre to the ridiculous – twenty-four eggs, cat's eyes – it's the stuff of farce.'

Nicholas shook his head. 'It's only half an hour from the assassination attempt and Colonel Baker knew.'

At the same time three of the Templars were entering the hotel. They were bedraggled and covered in snow. Four Swiss policemen were waiting for them in the reception area.

The Templars looked suitably abashed; they explained they had taken the Arab to the police station in Kloten. Before leaving they had phoned the police to ask them to be ready for their arrival. Unfortunately their Range Rover had hit ice just outside the hotel drive and skidded into a tree. In the confusion the Arab had escaped into the woods and the snow was so heavy that they had lost sight of him and his tracks were covered by the time they had recovered from their accident. Such was their explanation.

One of the policemen introduced himself. 'Very irregular proceeding – you should have waited for us to get here.'

One of the Templars answered, 'We didn't dare delay; we had no idea what support this assassin might have available.'

'Maybe,' answered the policeman, 'we shall have to await our tracker dogs to search the woods – difficult in this heavy snow.'

This was not only difficult but a waste of time. The Templars' accident had been faked and the Arab transported to the Templar Castle.

7

On arrival in London they went straight to the War Office. In spite of Nicholas uttering his password, they and their luggage were subjected to an exhaustive safety search. Once they were cleared, and their luggage stored, a woman army officer appeared to lead them to Colonel Baker's office.

He greeted them like old campaigners, shaking their hands and waving them towards some worn plastic-covered chairs arranged around a khaki-coloured metal table.

'Come and sit down and we'll get out of the way your signing of the Official Secrets Act. In a moment I'll introduce you to my PA, and she will bring us refreshments to revive you after your journey. She is *au fait* with the Templar case.'

They sat down and Colonel Baker put the documents in front of them. There was no further discussion. They looked at each other, nodded and signed. Colonel Baker witnessed their signatures, saying, 'I do not need to emphasise that the Official Secrets Act is binding, not only now, but after you are no longer involved. Permission would be needed to mention this case at any time.'

Colonel Baker looked at Theo. 'I can assure you your government is equally concerned. Anyway, enough of the obligations, you are now fully on board. Tell me about last night.'

'Before we do,' said Nicholas, 'we were staggered you knew about this attack so soon when you spoke to me on the phone last night. How come?'

'Nothing amazing – the Aljezur TV station had obviously been fed the news by Al Qaeda. It had been picked up as a news flash fifteen minutes after the incident.'

Colonel Baker did not add that a member of the Dolder Grand management was a British agent.

Tea arrived and was dispensed by Captain Patricia and each of them was given a plate of sandwiches containing hard cheese and dry ham. Patricia was a smart figure. Colonel Baker nodded to her. 'Our friends have "signed up".' Turning to the others: 'As you know by now, we have this somewhat eccentric password system and for you, Charlotte, yours is twenty-five eggs and Theo, twenty-six. Patricia is part of my Cat's-Eyes team; she is Cat's-Eyes two. If you can't get me in an emergency, ask for her.' Patricia smiled warmly at them. Theo hoped they would see more of her, he thought she was not only smart, but enticing.

Colonel Baker took a sip of tea and cleared his throat with a great harrumph. 'First I want to say how grateful we are to you all; you will be uniquely helpful as I believe you are all going back in June to the Templar Castle to do further research for them.'

Charlotte interrupted. 'We only received our invitations last night. I don't think any of us have accepted yet. I must say you seem to know everything just after it happens.'

Colonel Baker looked blandly at the ceiling. Patricia looked at her hands and smiled.

Colonel Baker continued unabashed.

'Well, let's rephrase that. We hope very much that you will accept their invitation as there is a great deal we have to know ... '

'Such as?' interrupted Theo.

Colonel Baker looked at Patricia. 'Perhaps you would like to come in here; we have listed our priorities this morning.'

She sat up straight and opening a file in front of her began to read out a set of questions.

'One – how large is the Order now in number of full members? Two – where are they planning to open new Commanderies? Three – do they publish accounts annually and what is their wealth? Four – there is a rumour that they are recruiting in Germany to form an associate order of New Teutonic Knights. We fear neo-Nazi elements are being attracted. Five – what is the involvement of Armenian Christians? We believe that the Bishop Krasnos you met last night has been excommunicated from the Armenian Church. The reason is somewhat obscure but he was said to be involved in a black mass ceremony involving young girls.'

'Holy cow!' Theo exclaimed.

Patricia blushed and paused. 'There are further details of an obscene nature which I would rather leave out.'

Nicholas winked at Theo and thought, 'What a swizz!'

'Very understandable,' said Colonel Baker, assuming a prudish expression. 'Carry on Patricia.'

She turned over her papers. 'Question number six – really the most important. What are they aiming for and how do they intend to achieve their ambitions? They state they wish to fulfil their traditional role of helping pilgrims going to the Holy Land. They have announced that they will help the funding of Christian shrines in Jerusalem – in addition they are planning to build a hospital there. Already they have been given some official status by the UN.'

Colonel Baker interrupted. 'We fear that their real aim is to foment outright war between Israel and the Arabs. We have information that they wish to control Jerusalem under a UN mandate. Their propaganda is increasingly strident. They are obviously well funded. Only a few of their members are allowed to give interviews and their answers are stereotyped. Their answers come off pat. We've got to realise that the Middle East is a powder keg and if these Templar Johnnies are going to throw a lighted match into their keg – who knows what might happen?'

'What sort of match?' asked Theo, looking at Colonel Baker, who was silent for a moment.

'Well, an assassination, carried out by a Templar but made

to look as if it was of Jewish or Arab origin. Or maybe a sacrilegious attack on Jewish, Christian or Muslim shrines, but made to look as if from their enemies, such as the Wailing Wall in Jerusalem, so sacred to Jews; the Holy Sepulchre for Christians or an attack on the Muslim shrine in Mecca – any of these could be the spark and similar attempts have been made before. There was a genuine plan some years ago by young Jewish zealots to bomb the Temple Mount Mosque; the last attempt was abandoned because they could not get a Jewish Rabbi to bless their scheme.'

Colonel Baker let out a guffaw of laughter. 'Ridiculous, but just think of the result if they had succeeded: they wanted to start the third world war. Next question Patricia ... '

She continued. 'Question number seven – what is the real power of the Grand Master? These Templars have all the qualities of being cult members revolving around a charismatic leader. His origins are obscure, yet he has quickly become a powerful international figure. What is the psychological profile of this man?'

Colonel Baker interrupted again. 'He is not a giggly, immoral cult leader like that ridiculous Indian Maharashi; nor a mad power-crazed individual like the American evangelist, Jones, who persuaded his followers to commit mass suicide, nor a Hitler with his crazed racial visions of world domination – no! He is a man using religion, Holy Grail hocus pocus, to dominate his followers. There is even the ridiculous claim by his mother that he was miraculously conceived by an angel.'

At this, Nicholas raised his eyebrows. 'Sounds familiar!'

Colonel Baker powered on. 'What disturbs us is that he evidently has a hidden agenda, that he has an exceedingly powerful control over his Templar members, that he can sway crowds, and that power feeds back to him so that, like all cult leaders, his ego seems to grow, fed by constant adulation.

'To sum up: we fear this movement could destabilise further an already unstable world, especially in the Middle East.

'Nearer home we fear that the young and impressionable are being brainwashed; these Templars are now actively recruiting in the better universities. To try and get inside information we had two of our agents accepted: one of them became converted into the cult and betrayed our attempt to infiltrate the movement; the other had a breakdown but we were able to learn that if he revealed anything of their secrets the punishment would be burial alive. He committed suicide three months ago. It seems that there is some strong psychological pressure of a perverse nature, forcing members into a profound change of character, possibly via drugs and repetitive corrupt practices of a deviant sort – just the sort of behaviour that the original Templars were accused of, which was used as an excuse to extinguish the Order in the fourteenth century.'

Colonel Baker paused for a moment. 'As you know, I have this hang-up that they have got close to overcoming old age, hence my wish to involve you in the "Eau de Cologne" experiment. By the way, did it have any effect on the so-called Karl?'

Theo nodded, 'You certainly hit the jackpot.'

They then described his collapse at the symposium.

Colonel Baker sat silently for a moment and drummed his fingers on the table.

'My God, what a powerful hold that would give them if it turns out to be possible.'

'How?' asked Charlotte.

For a moment they sat quietly.

Colonel Baker lowered his voice, as if reluctant to answer and appear foolish.

'One of the rumours about the original Templars was that they were overcoming the ageing process, and there's a similar rumour circulating about the inner elite of these new Templars. This does not have to be due to the black arts; many scientists are doing intense research, studying matters like the secret of the Methuselah worm with its excessive longevity and on the amazing jelly fish, Territopsis Nutricala, which reverts to youthful form once it has mated.'

Theo let out one of his laughs. 'I like the idea of that. Wow!' Charlotte and Patricia blushed. The Colonel ignored this interruption and continued.

'Like many other cults the leaders seem to have the power to sexually enslave. The Grand Master is said to have a corps of attractive women close to him and there are some pretty unsavoury rumours circulating. We have a conviction that we do not have much time. These Templars are raising their profile and spreading their Jerusalem propaganda, plus publicising the scandal of Bethlehem being cut off by the appalling mega-wall the Israelis have built. We've got to get to the truth of what is going on and need information from insiders who are unlikely to be brainwashed. This is why your return to do research for them would be an ideal opportunity for us to learn more. This assassination attempt is providing worldwide publicity and raising the Grand Master to the status of a possible future martyr on a world stage. Will you help us?'

For a moment the three of them were silent as the gravity of their task became apparent. Their invitation to return to Switzerland in June began to seem threatening.

Colonel Baker added, 'By the way, we will give you anti-brainwashing techniques and stimulating drugs to avoid you being hypnotised – I think that's the most you will be threatened with.'

Nicholas raised his hand. 'I'm sure we want to help you, but could you give us a room where the three of us can discuss the issues?'

Colonel Baker said, 'Of course. Patricia, could you find them a room? I think Brigadier Jackson's will be free; he's in Afghanistan this week. When you have finished ring me on extension 579.'

He looked peeved. Nicholas was reminded of his house-master at school when he had to tell him he did not like playing cricket.

Brigadier Jackson's office was a complete contrast to Colonel Baker's austere quarters. There was a large sofa and two easy chairs covered in flowery chintz. The walls were covered with pictures of tanks and regimental parades. There was a large picture of the Brigadier on a horse next to the Queen, similarly mounted.

The three sat and discussed what they had learnt. They agreed that the scenario painted by Colonel Baker seemed far-fetched. There did not seem to have been any illegality in the operations of these new Templars, though maybe there was unhealthy pressure on young aspirants to commit themselves to the Order. However, they agreed they were still interested to learn more of the research the Templars required of them in June, as it might reveal knowledge useful to their academic careers. The financial incentives were also tempting.

Nicholas rang the Colonel's extension and told him they had agreed under certain conditions, for instance they didn't want to go as far as bugging rooms or microfilming documents.

There was a pause and Nicholas could hear the Colonel drumming his fingers on the table.

'Come and explain, but I think we should not lose the opportunity to get information from inside their head-quarters.'

When they rejoined Colonel Baker he still looked a little peeved when they repeated their decision.

'Not a hundred per cent, but better than nothing.' He picked up his phone. 'Patricia, get a date for our friends to

have a day of anti-brainwashing and anti-hypnosis training.'
He stood up. 'Thank you for coming and agreeing to help.
We shall continue to build up our information here and
arrange to meet before you leave for Switzerland in June.'

When they re-entered the outside world of London after
their meeting they felt a mood of anti-climax, but they
expressed pleasure at the prospect of meeting again in June.
Theo took his leave of them to go to a hotel close to the
British Museum, where he was to spend a few days
researching before returning to America. Nicholas asked
Charlotte whether she would like to join him for tea but she
declined, saying she was going to get a train to Worcester to
stay for two days at a convent where one of the sisters was a
Shroud expert. He was even more peeved when she added
that she was going to be away from Cambridge during the
coming term as she had been promised access to the Shroud
Institute in Turin, where they had promised to show her
new scientific evidence.

Nicholas felt deflated being left to find his own way back
to Cambridge alone. As they stood on the steps of the War
Office, she was sensitive to his feelings and kissed him
warmly before getting into a taxi. Nicholas leant through
the open window and said, 'Remember you are coming to
the Michaelhouse May Ball with me.'

'Of course,' she said, 'I think of nothing else.'

That cheered him.

8

The three of them did not speak again until the middle of
the summer term after they each had had a letter from the
Templar Grand Master, delivered personally by a Templar
messenger. To Nicholas it came by hand via the unwelcome
visit of the English Templar Master, Sir Darcy de Malplaquet. His unannounced arrival at Nicholas's college came
just as he was about to go out to lunch with a potential
publisher. His telephone rang in his room. It was the
porter's lodge.

'Two gentlemen here to see you, sir. A Sir Darcy and a
companion – says he has something he must give you
personally.'

'Oh hell,' muttered Nicholas. 'Better send them over.'

Nicholas heard him through his open window tapping his
silver-topped cane as he walked towards his staircase, and
then tapping each stair as he came up to his door. Nicholas
thought of Blind Pew in *Treasure Island*, and shivered. He
opened his door.

'What a surprise, what brings you here?'

The visitors swept into the room and de Malplaquet per-
formed a heel-clicking routine. 'You remember Fred; he was
with us that night in Zurich when the assassination attempt
destroyed the evening. We have a letter to give you.'

Nicholas offered them sherry but explained that he would
need to go to an appointment very shortly.

Malplaquet nodded. 'Do you have a beer for Fred? Sherry
is bad for his liver.' Fred blushed.

Nicholas replied that he would have to get the beer from
the buttery but before that he poured himself and his visitor
their sherry. His visitor clinked his glass with him.

'How very kind.'

Nicholas had been playing his Gilbert and Sullivan as a gentle background to his morning and went to turn it off.

'Please leave that on. I adore G and S,' said Malplaquet.

When Nicholas returned with the beer, he found them kneeling in front of his CD player, examining it closely. They stood up rather guiltily as he entered.

'Very droll our G and S, though Fred thinks them thoroughly incomprehensible – oh dear – our younger generation. Anyway, thank you for your hospitality and for receiving us without warning, but last night I received a messenger from Zurzach carrying a letter for you from the Grand Master. It is *de rigueur* for us to deliver the Grand Master's letters immediately by hand, so Fred and I drove from our new Commanderie at Temple Guiting. We've come, as is our custom, *tout de suite* – don't you know?'

The whole matter was so bizarre that Nicholas was temporarily lost for words but eventually said, 'You seem to have gone to a great deal of trouble. Fred, here's your beer and Darcy, will you have another sherry?' Fred opened his tin of beer and, ignoring the glass that Nicholas had placed nearby, began to slurp directly from the can. 'I am a little short of time. You mentioned a letter.'

Malplaquet put his sherry down and placed a slim black leather document case on a low coffee table; the case was embossed in gold with the Templar insignia. Although it was a warm day, he was wearing a waistcoat and through one of the buttonholes a gold chain was fixed. With a flourish he pulled this out and at one end was a key with which he opened the document case. From this he pulled out a stiff cream envelope addressed to Nicholas. It was sealed with wax on which the Templar insignia was impressed.

'Shall I open this now?' asked Nicholas.

'Of course! I must explain the Grand Master never communicates by telephone, fax or email. All these media can be tapped or imitated. All his messages and commands are conveyed only in this way by personal delivery and sealed with the Templar seal.'

'Good heavens,' exclaimed Nicholas, 'unique in this day and age of email communication. Did someone ride day and night from Zurzach just to give it to you to give it to me today? I am overwhelmed!'

Malplaquet ignored the irony in Nicholas's questioning.

'Of course, it is the correct way for our Grand Master to communicate. He has staff to issue the mundane orders of the day but to ensure direct contact the delivery of sealed letters is his august way. I should add they only go to those important in his eyes.'

Nicholas filled up their glasses and gave Fred another can of beer. 'Thank you. I am deeply honoured. Can I read it now?'

Malplaquet nodded vigorously.

Nicholas slit open the letter; he had to admit the whole charade of personal delivery was impressive, conveying an aura of the illustrious importance of the sender. The letter said that the Grand Master hoped that Nicholas would come to Switzerland to do research in the long vacation at their castle in Zurzach. The Grand Master looked forward to spending time discussing the history of the Order with him. He would be directed by their chief librarian, the Grand Duke Alexei Popov.

On acceptance of this invitation he would receive a prepayment of eight thousand pounds. Nicholas was staggered at the amount. He looked at Malplaquet.

'Do I reply now?'

The monetary promise contained in the letter put the need to leave for his meeting to one side.

'Of course, please reply now so that it may be conveyed back in the same manner, by hand. It's the customary way we exchange correspondence with the Grand Master.'

Nicholas immediately went to his desk and on College note-paper accepted the offer with expressions of enthusiasm and thanks. He put this reply in an envelope and handed it to them.

'Could you please address this correctly and please excuse me as I must go now to my appointment.' He opened his arms wide to shepherd them out of the door.

Malplaquet clicked his heels and nodded to Fred to follow him; they seemed reluctant to leave.

'Dear Nicholas, such a pleasure to meet you again in your charming and intimate College. I might see you again in Switzerland when you are there this summer, though I am very busy overseeing our renovation works at our commanderie at Temple Guiting.'

Later that day Nicholas heard from Charlotte in Turin and Theo from Harvard that they had received similar letters, personally delivered. Charlotte had been surprised to be visited by a very elegant French lady while studying some documents in Turin Cathedral. She had introduced herself as the Countess de Poitier; she had dyed blue-grey hair tied back in a tight bun; it was difficult to estimate her age. Her approach was aloof. Charlotte found herself reacting negatively and asked how the French woman knew she was to be found in the Cathedral treasury. To this question she gave the unsatisfactory answer.

'Évidemment.'

Afterwards Charlotte felt uneasy, as if she was under constant observation. She had received the same message as Nicholas and was also required to answer immediately. She thought the whole process bizarre and unsettling.

Theo, in America, received his message from an exuberant banker from Wall Street who treated him to an elaborate lunch in one of Harvard's most expensive restaurants. Theo was amazed by the monetary reward and unruffled by the mode in which the offer was conveyed. When discussing this with Nicholas, he commented that this personal delivery performance was a subtle public relations exercise, displaying extravagance in the expense involved and giving an aura of power and mystery. His Wall Street messenger had told him that the Templars were well on the way to achieving major UN mission status in the Holy Land.

A week later, by normal postal means, they received a letter from the chief librarian of the Templar Order, Count Alexei Popov. The letter informed them that he would be acting as their director of studies. To each he set out the area of investigation required from them.

For Theo, the task was to prove the reality of the Holy Grail and its discovery by the early Templars when they had first arrived in Jerusalem. He would then trace the eventual journey of the Grail after the Templar Order was suppressed.

Of Nicholas they required that he study historical rumours that some of the fleeing Templars from La Rochelle reached Mexico when the Order was suppressed in 1309. He would also be required to investigate the transformation of the Portuguese Templars into the Order of Christ.

Charlotte's task was to prove the past Templar ownership of the Shroud of Turin and trace its connection with various representations of the head of Christ found in Templar castles in the Middle Ages.

Nicholas was delighted to think that the three of them would be together again in Switzerland. He also welcomed the idea of a break from College politics. He was continually being dragged into the feud between the Master and the Chaplain; the latter was claiming to be close to a breakdown. Every year they celebrated with a feast and a special mass in the College Chapel, the memory of their famous Tudor student, John Cardinal Fisher, later to be martyred by Henry VIII. This celebration took place every year on 6 July, this being his saint's day in the Anglican calendar. As the Catholic Church celebrated St John Fisher's feast day on

22 June, along with that of Sir Thomas More, Francis thought it would be a good ecumenical move to invite the Chaplain of Fisher House to preach the sermon.

The Master had seen the proof of the proposed order of service but on spotting the name of Father Alban from Fisher House as the preacher, had summoned his Chaplain to his room. This meeting had ended in a shouting match with the Master forbidding the Catholic University Chaplain entering the College Chapel to give a sermon. Father Francis had pointed out that their neighbour, Trinity College, and several other Cambridge Colleges, were happy to have Catholic masses in their chapels.

This elicited the response, 'I'm having no bloody Papist preaching in my Chapel!'

After this meeting Father Francis asked Nicholas if he could have a day out with him at his cottage in Madingley.

It had been a long day for Nicholas.

9

At the beginning of the long vacation in June they were summoned by Colonel Baker to attend a day's instruction on brainwashing techniques and the necessary psychological and medical protection they might require during their time with the Templars. This would take place at the War Office.

When they arrived they were met by Captain Patricia, who led them to a lecture room, where Colonel Baker and two middle-aged men in white coats awaited them.

Colonel Baker introduced them as specialists in the Army Medical Corps. He thanked Captain Patricia by gently patting her bottom as she turned away. She looked back and smiled.

'That's a smile of love,' thought Charlotte.

Colonel Baker set out their programme. He would first describe the latest findings on brainwashing and then cover hypnotic attempts to alter people's opinions. After that the Medical Corps officers would describe, in more depth, physical and mental reactions to brainwashing and hypnotic influences.

Colonel Baker smiled at them all and said, 'Before starting, I want to tell you you are now officially Acting Lieutenants. Welcome to your new status.' He smiled benignly as he went to each one of them and shook their hands. 'The bonus is you will get a Lieutenant's pay while you are working for us.'

Nicholas interrupted. 'I'm sure I speak for us all that this is totally unexpected and most welcome; however if our investigations last until normal military retiring age, will we get pensions?' He said this with a perfectly straight face. The doctors looked aghast. Charlotte laughed out loud and Theo guffawed, 'That's our boy.'

Colonel Baker pursed his lips and frowned. 'Ever the joker, Nicholas. Let's have less of the acting and more of the Lieutenant. If you don't come up with the goods we require from Zurzach you will get a court martial long before a pension. Now I should like to begin. At the end of each quarter of an hour I'll pause for questions – sensible questions, Nicholas!'

He began by describing the emergence of what had become brainwashing in the Korean War and how this became an explanation for the breakdown of some American troops. These breakdowns had been attributed to fiendish psychological pressure leading to permanent change of character. Colonel Baker said this explanation was false. Up-to-date research showed that these behavioural changes were mostly caused by sleep deprivation over an extended period, followed by unpleasant torture to get the unfortunate prisoners to conform to the views of their captors. The Colonel backed up this theory by distributing a series of written reports on individual cases. They proved that once the captives had returned to their home countries and after special care, they would revert to their former thought systems. The second half of his lecture dealt with the effect of hypnosis. He said it was not possible to influence a captive permanently and hypnosis always needed the co-operation of the subject. During his talk he dealt peremptorily with their questions. At the end of his lecture he slowly closed his folder of notes and, without speaking, looked at them intently. He was silent for what seemed a long period, then said, 'How do we explain some definite cases of what could be permanent brainwashing of some people who have expressed opposition to these so-called Templars? How do we explain the effectiveness of Templar indoctrination of those entering the Order on trial? We know that some extreme religious sects achieve this over a period of time, but not on outsiders opposed to them.

'I give you a most recent occurrence – happening to someone we all know.' He paused dramatically. 'This someone was that excitable Welsh Professor, Darren Jones, who caused such a rumpus at the Templar seminar in Zurich, claiming the true Holy Grail was in the possession of the Powell family in Wales.' There was another dramatic pause. 'He has now renounced that theory and is backing the Templar claims that they possess it in their Armenian monastery.'

The three academics all exclaimed with noises of disbelief.

Theo gasped, 'Unbelievable – that silly old Welshman was obsessed with his theory. When did you learn this? My internet search engine would have picked up any public statement by him.'

Colonel Baker smiled smugly. 'We have inside information at the university presses. We get first-hand knowledge of any publications concerning matters of interest to us – cults in general and their various beliefs. The Oxford University Press has told us a paper is to be published next month by Professor Jones, based on research he has carried out recently at the Temple Castle in Zurzach. The University Press is not letting out the news until the date of publication and with its launch will be maximum publicity, TV and the press etcetera.'

Charlotte turned to the others. 'Research at the Templar Castle by Darren Jones! That's ridiculous; I don't think he would ever set foot in that place after his treatment at the seminar.'

'I agree,' said the Colonel, 'so the question is why did he go there, and what made him change his views? Is he brainwashed to the extent of denying his life's work? We have here a case of pure brainwashing. We need urgently to find out how this was achieved. We can't let the Templars loose entertaining politicians and leaders in many fields, if the Templars have perfected some drug or system that enables them to permanently change an individual's firmly held convictions. We have a nightmare scenario here. So the first thing you can help us with is to find out, from Darren Jones, how this change came about. Theo, I think this falls to you as this is also your field of study; perhaps if you could arrange to speak to him on the pretext of comparing notes on the seminar in Zurich, he might let you know as a fellow academic that he has changed his views, and why.'

Theo nodded. 'I have his telephone number – why don't we call him now?'

They all agreed. The Colonel said they would record the conversation. Recording it proved, in the event, to be a waste of time. Theo made immediate contact. He asked him if he was well and what was his considered opinion of the seminar after his unpleasant treatment by the Templars. The Professor just laughed; the Templars, he said, had kindly made up for it by giving him very generous hospitality and free range of their library to do further research. He confirmed he would shortly be publishing his conclusions in a paper being released by the Oxford University Press. He did not reveal what those conclusions were save for hinting that they would surprise them all.

After the conversation with Darren Jones they had a break for another sandwich lunch in Colonel Baker's office. Following this the doctors took over and explained that each would have medicals and psychological tests and after this would be prescribed their antidotes individually so they could resist any possible brainwashing or being in some way drugged if they were to be alone with any of the Templars in the castle. They were assured that their antidotes were totally safe but would have the effect of taking a strong cup of caffeine which could cause insomnia; for this they would be given effective sleeping pills.

At the conclusion of their tests they all gathered again in Colonel Baker's office. He told them to return in a week's time when they would have their antidotes ready and they would be issued with special mobile phones. These would enable them to scramble their calls and would be programmed to reach him wherever he was. He said he would not see them on their return but wished them every success in their investigations.

10

At the beginning of June they made their way to London City Airport via the War Office where they picked up their phones and various pills from Captain Patricia.

As they boarded their plane they all entertained feelings of keen anticipation. Both the men looked forward to facing the intellectual challenge of examining the Templars' claims, which they believed were based entirely on supposition and wishful interpretation of historical rumours. Charlotte's sense of anticipation was accompanied by an elusive feeling of unease; to her the Shroud of Turin was a sacred object, and the desire of the Templars to try and prove historical ownership appeared to be a curious task. Even if that could be proved, what did they intend to do with such a fact?

Their plane for Zurich left on time from the uncluttered London City Airport and landed at the efficient machine of Kloten Airport in Zurich.

As they came into the arrivals hall, they saw two of the Indians from the seminar holding a board with their names on it. On this occasion they were wearing long grey Indian jackets with the Templar insignia embossed in gold on their breast pockets. On seeing them they burst into smiling greetings of, 'Welcome, welcome. How good to see you again.' They put their hands together and gave them a namostar's greeting, bowing low towards them before taking charge of their bags. They went outside the terminal and a large black Mercedes glided up. It had such dark tinted glass they could hardly see the driver inside, so that it gave the impression it could have come to them by remote control. All three of them were directed to sit in the back of the car. One of the Indians gave each of them an envelope, shut the doors and got in the front with the driver. He then turned round and slid back the dividing glass, separating them from the front.

'We shall arrive at our castle in about an hour so enjoy the drive.'

The envelopes contained a letter of welcome from the Templar chief librarian, Count Alexis. It informed them that they would be staying at the Park Hotel in the town of Zurzach, where they could also enjoy the attached spa. He would come to them that evening at five o'clock and then take them to the Templars' castle where they would have time to be introduced to the library and the layout of those parts of the building that were open to them. The letter went on to say that they were invited to a reception which was going to be given by the Grand Master to honour a visit from a delegation of Teutonic Knights; jacket and ties requested.

Nicholas read the reference to the Teutonic Knights and snorted with derision. 'My God! These resurrected medieval orders are popping up like autumn mushrooms.'

They found their hotel agreeable and efficient in its Swiss ambience. They gathered in the hall at five o'clock to await the arrival of their mentor, Count Alexis. He came through the door of the hotel as nearby church clocks were striking the hour. He was a tall, commanding figure, and though dressed in the Templar uniform, was also sporting black Cossack boots. He had well-groomed, blond hair, a swarthy complexion and a copious blond beard. He went to each one of them, bowed his head curtly, before cupping their out-stretched hands with both of his and saying, 'May our God bless you. Come follow me.' As later events unfolded, the significance of his expression 'our God' took on a darker meaning. He swept them out of the door and took them to another large Mercedes. He directed the two men to the back and led Charlotte to sit beside him in the front.

'Good, modern Swiss hotel, I think. Pity about all the fat walruses in the spa pool – people like that should only swim in tent-like costumes, like Victorians.' He slapped his thigh and roared with laughter, at the same time glancing at Charlotte, who smiled politely in return. He switched on the engine and revved it up before leaving the front of the hotel, with tyres screaming as he swept on to the road. He drove through the small town of Zurzach and raced at speed up its main road, leaving a blurred impression of a pleasant town with churches, shops and fine domestic buildings. At the top of the town the road looped up the hill and into the country-side beyond, where after a few minutes they turned right on to a tree-lined avenue. After a mile they reached an imposing entrance gate with two small towers on either side; they had arrived at the Templar Castle. The Count pointed an electronic gate opener and they drove on, passing white-railed fields in which well-groomed horses grazed. At the end of this avenue the Castle stood four square, surrounded by a large moat. It was substantial and equal in size to the front of Buckingham Palace. It was built of stone in the fourteenth century. On one side of it was attached a large round building with a high tiled roof, most of it surrounded by the large moat. It had a few narrow windows thirty feet above the ground. The severity of the building was offset by a dozen flagpoles on its roof, colourful flags fluttering in the wind.

The car slowed to a stop and the Count, pointing proudly at the Castle, said, 'Quite a building. You know of course the Templars created Switzerland after the suppression of our Order, the Swiss became famed as mercenaries, some of them being snapped up by the Pope to become his Swiss guards in their Michelangelo dolls' clothes.' The Count roared with laughter and patted Charlotte's thigh by way of self-applause. His exposition was interrupted by the arrival of a bus hooting its horn behind them. The Count muttered a curse and again revved up the car engine before surging forward. They drove round to the back of the Castle where there were some thirty cars parked in front of a large range of stables, garages and outbuildings. The Count parked his car near two Maybach limousines being cleaned by the Indians. One of the cars had the Templar insignia, the two horsemen on one steed, etched on its doors. This insignia of the Templars, which was originally to signify their poverty, was incongruous on such a vehicle. As they got out of the Count's car the Indians waved at them and smiled, one of them exclaiming, 'This is Grand Master Sahib's car.' As he said this, the large bus came round the side of the Castle and parked near them.

The Count ushered them towards an imposing entrance where a high double door was opened between two granite pillars. Behind them, the bus was unloading its contents. Thirty men lined up in three lines of ten as if in a military platoon – all were dressed in black shirts and wide black leather riding breeches tucked into shiny riding boots. They were being lined up by a man with red epaulettes on his shoulders, marshalling them into position with a black riding crop. All had shaven heads. The Teutonic Knights had arrived. The academics paused in the doorway and regarded this visitation with expressions of puzzlement.

The Count smiled. 'Our Teutonic brothers have arrived for the party – the Huns always overdo it. They call themselves "The New Knights of Prussia", known in the trade as "The Knops", but we just call them "Teutonic".'

Nicholas replied, 'We suffered in the thirties with similarly dressed members led by an unpleasant fascist leader, Oswald Mosley. I hope your brothers have leanings of a more liberal sort; their appearance is rather daunting.'

The Count laughed. 'Nonsense. Good fellows after a drink! Follow me.'

He led them through the doors into a stone-floored corridor running the length of the building to the left and right. The Count led them nearly to the end of the corridor and stopped at a door; this was about ten feet tall and opened to reveal a magnificent library in a room one hundred feet long with a beamed roof thirty feet above them.

The Count pointed to some of the shelves which were empty and explained that they had discovered woodworm and that the books had been removed to other rooms in the Castle. These books were being sorted as it was planned to furnish a library in a school they were opening near Zurich. The Count turned to them and said, 'This school will be first-rate with wonderful facilities. We are being helped in the sorting of the books by a charming young American librarian, also from your Harvard University. Like you she's here for a few weeks in her vacation – of Scandinavian origin. You'll meet her very shortly at the party, Kirsten Olsen by name.'

Theo's eyes sparkled. 'I know her by sight. She works in the Harvard main library; she's a knockout, a stunner.' He let out one of his whooping laughs, which automatically caused them all to join in.

The library was impressive and seemed well organised. In the middle of the wall opposite the entrance door were large floor-length windows looking out on to an inner cloister. On the floor of this courtyard were a line of tombstones lying flat on the ground. The Count explained that these stones were of thirteenth-century origin and below them generations of Knights Templars were buried. They spent some ten minutes examining the books in their shelves, and also various journals laid out on a line of tables which had comfortable leather chairs beside them. The Count stood looking out of the windows while they did this but after a quarter of an hour gave a discreet cough, saying, 'It's time we joined the party. Follow me.'

They began walking down the corridor and passed another set of large double doors where the corridor took a sharp right turn.

The Count pointed to the doors. 'That is the way into our

Church – the round building you saw outside. As you know, many of our Templar churches were round, like the ones you have in London and Cambridge. I'm afraid ours is reserved only for members of the knighthood, but we do have a ecumenical gathering on Sunday.'

While he was speaking, a door further down the corridor opened and a column of the Teutonic Knights appeared and, at a quick march, walked away from them.

The Count beckoned to them. 'Come on, quick, otherwise the Huns will drink all the drink and eat all the food.'

They set off in quick pursuit and reached a grand staircase where other guests were ascending. At the top they were led through elaborately carved doors held open by two young Templars. Inside they found another medieval hall, heavily beamed like the library. The walls were hung with ancient heraldic shields and weapons; large swords and pikes were fancily hung in circles, and below these, several suits of armour decorated with the Templar insignia. The entrance of the crowd into the hall was slow, as inside the Grand Master was being introduced to each guest. A Templar assistant enquired the name of everyone as they came forward, looked at his list and then whispered the information to the Grand Master.

Templar guests went down on one knee as they faced the Master and kissed the ring on his right hand. When Nicholas and Theo saw this happening in front of them, Theo exclaimed, 'I'm not playing that ego game; even bishops have given that up so I'll crush his hand with my baseballer's grip.'

Charlotte overheard this. 'Well I think I'll try and impress him with the curtsy I perfected in my part in the ADC last summer – that should give me Brownie points,' she giggled. 'What about you, Nick?'

'I shall give a curt bow and confuse him by my perfected Freemason's squeezing of his index finger – let's see what he makes of that!'

In front of them the Teutonic Knights had formed a single line as they approached their host. As they were introduced they bowed their heads and clicked their heels before making a clenched-fist salute, and then resting an open hand on their heart. To each the Grand Master spoke softly in German and then lifted his ring finger which they all kissed as they left him to go into the hall.

Charlotte approached him first, and curtsied as she had promised. The Grand Master expressed enchantment and, putting his hands on her shoulders, helped her up, saying, 'I look forward to seeing more of you during your research here.' She moved away before he could proffer his ring.

Nicholas approached next, and as a hand came forward he languidly took it and lifted it up, studied the ring, and said, 'Amazing! I have a similar ring I bought in Istanbul.'

The Grand Master raised his eyebrows. 'This one we know belonged to one of our illustrious Grand Masters, and I suspect yours is smaller.'

Nicholas smiled sweetly. 'Actually I think mine is bigger.' So saying he took the Master's hand and gave him his pseudo-Freemason handshake and moved away. As he joined the crowd he heard a yelp from the Grand Master and Theo saying, 'Sorry, it's my baseball playing responsible for overdoing my handshakes – truly sorry.'

The three quickly made their way to the far end of the room, where food and drink were being dispensed from an immensely long table. Here they found Count Alexis holding out his glass over the table for more vodka; he had already sunk two glasses. The majority of the other guests were drinking brandy and champagne cocktails, and the volume of voices was rising noticeably. Taking a cocktail each, Nicholas and Charlotte went over to talk to him. They were intrigued to see him in earnest conversation with the beautiful companion of the Grand Master, who was with him at the Zurich symposium the night he was attacked.

The Count introduced her to them as Lady Natasha. She looked openly uninterested when they told her the reason for their return and shortly excused herself to leave them and join the Grand Master.

Charlotte asked the Count whether she was married to an English lord with her title or had been knighted for some reason. The Count by then was on his fourth vodka and laughed loudly.

'Yes! Yes! Nighted, not knighted by the Grand Master. Actually Templar full members are entitled to take the prefix of Sir or Lady in their own right.' He laughed again and pinched her bottom.

Nicholas took Charlotte's arm and led her away to join Theo, who was talking to a blonde girl. They discovered this was the American librarian whom Theo knew from Harvard. Theo introduced her as Kirsten and they all enjoyed sharing their experiences of the Templars and immediately judged that she would be good company. Theo explained to them that she was staying at a different hotel, high up in the town, called the Zurzacherhof. Although it was nice she was finding it spoilt by the presence of the Teutonic Knights staying there, drinking heavily and singing German songs late each night. The three invited her to join them for dinner and she enthusiastically accepted.

Silence now spread through the room as the Grand Master had mounted a platform in the middle of the hall. Another Templar was calling for silence. The Grand Master began speaking slowly in his deep, sonorous voice. He told them that the clouds of war were threatening in the Middle East and that the Order had a great task ahead of it. It needed new members to strengthen it and he was pleased to announce that they were coming forward in growing numbers to join in their sacred work. He went on to welcome the Teutonic Knights, who had already established a mission in Egypt and were helping the Coptic Church, members of which were constantly harassed by Muslim extremists. 'In Jerusalem we have founded a hospital; likewise our brothers the Teutonic Knights have founded one in Cairo. Similar to our founding our college near Zurich, they will be starting one in Egypt.' These announcements led to rapturous applause punctuated with cries of 'Sieg Heil' from the Teutonic Knights.

The Grand Master continued, 'I should like you now to greet Pastor Bob McPherson. He is a right-hand man to the famous Pastor John Hagee, the well-known US television evangelist. Unfortunately we are running short of time for, as you know, it is a strict rule of our Order that after seven o'clock, only Templars are allowed in our houses to prepare for the "Great Silence of the Night". Pastor Hagee is rallying thousands of American Christians to face the coming struggle between good and evil. Pastor Bob is close to him, and as a member of US Templars Inc., we welcome him.' Further rapturous applause and cheers from the Templars. The Grand Master went on, 'As you probably know, the famous John Hagee, a friend to President Bush, is also head of "Christians United for Israel". I now ask Pastor Bob to tell us more of this organisation.'

The applause that followed was somewhat muted, there was a general air of puzzlement, save from the Teutonic Knights, who were scowling. 'Christians United for Israel' was not a concept they found easy to accept.

Pastor Bob mounted the platform. He wore a white suit, a purple shirt under a dog collar and a silver cross on a cord around his neck. He bowed his head in prayer and his lips moved silently. He then looked up and smiled cherubically.

'Brothers and sisters in God, I bring you great news from "Christians United for Israel". Christian Zionism is an exploding movement in these troubled times – these end times! Israel's sufferings fulfil biblical prophecy and are the forerunner of Armageddon and the Second Coming.

' "Christians United for Israel" links hundreds of evangelical leaders. Pastor Hagee is one of Israel's most influential supporters. Outside his church in Texas we have a copy of the Wailing Wall and inside we fly the Israeli flag. Prime Minister Ehud visited us when he was Mayor of Jerusalem, so you see we are taken seriously and we are seeking a showdown with Islam. I quote Pastor Hagee, "This is a religious war that Islam cannot and must not win. The end of the world is rapidly approaching – rejoice and be exceedingly glad, the best is yet to be." ' Pastor Bob joined his hands as if in prayer. 'That is the message I wish you to take with you tonight.'

Theo turned to the others and whispered, 'What frightening evangelical rant. I hope we are spared the Rapture rubbish.'

A Teutonic Knight standing next to him nodded in agreement. He was obviously the worse for drink and shouted out, 'Sieg Heil', and was joined by the other Teutonic Knights in the room.

The sermonising pastor looked astounded. The Grand Master reacted rapidly and stepped into his place. The partygoers fell silent. The Castle bell struck its three-quarter-hour chime and resolved the tension in the hall. The Grand Master raised his hand.

'I'm afraid we do not have time for our traditional prayers in which no doubt Pastor Bob would have liked to have shared, but as I told you at the beginning, all must leave the Castle before the clock strikes seven, so we only have time for our traditional St Bernard blessing, the inspiration of our Order in its infancy.' He repeated the prayer they had heard that evening in the Zurich hotel, where the assassination attempt had taken place.

As they started leaving, alarm bells rang throughout the Castle. Kirsten, their new librarian friend, told them this happened every evening, giving a warning that the Castle had to be empty of visitors.

They found Count Alexis holding on to a pillar by the front door, obviously necessary after the amount of vodka he had consumed. When he saw them he told them he had arranged for a car to take them back to the hotel, excusing himself by saying that he had to continue entertaining the Teutonic Knights.

At that moment, one of the Indians got out of another large Mercedes and waved at them as they stood in the door-way. The four of them agreed not to discuss the evening as they were driven back to their hotel, but Theo could not help saying, 'Sieg Heil – I ask you? That pastor looked as if he had entered a completely mad dream.' Theo began his infectious laughter, which they all joined in. The Indian driver looked round anxiously as if he had a load of lunatics to transport.

Over dinner in the hotel they found that Kirsten would add to the pleasure of their time as researchers, and fuelled with good Swiss wine, the ebullient mood continued. Kirsten was delighted to have found sympathetic companions, as she had been left to her own devices in the evenings. Nicholas asked her to give her impression of the Templars and whether she had yet been under any pressure to join them. She told them that she had been interviewed in Harvard before her vacation job was confirmed. She had, however, been asked by the Count whether she would like to learn more about the Templar Order but as far as she could see, the members seemed to be following a curious cult of medieval hocus pocus imbued with a heavy, emotional, evangelical fervour. She had also told the Count that her mother was Jewish and she herself followed a liberal Jewish life. For a moment she was distracted by Theo interrupting – he was already sufficiently smitten to want to learn more about her.

'Although you have a Swedish father, do you feel different from them when you meet his side of the family?'

Kirsten smiled. 'Do you mean summer Swedes, or winter Swedes? They are two different races: the summer ones – extrovert, the winter ones – mega-introverts. I like them

most in the summer version and can identify with them.'
She went back to discussing the Templars and told them
how she had been invited by the Count to a Templar
ceremony in the chapel on her first Sunday in Zurzach.
The first part of the ceremony had been one of rousing
hymn singing, followed by a long sermon about protecting
the Holy Land. However, the end of the ceremony was of a
total different character. The Grand Master had entered,
robed in a magnificent high-collared cope, preceded by four
acolytes carrying candles, and behind them, a monstrance
carried under a gold and silk cover, accompanied by two
white-robed female Templars, swinging censers producing
copious clouds of incense. The monstrance was placed on the
altar. Kirsten continued by emphasising that this procession
created a complete change in the emotional atmosphere, from
a service of evangelical sing-along, to one of strange mystery.
The Grand Master had stood at the altar with his back to
them, so that his head was completely hidden from them by
the high collar of his cope. As he bowed and knelt he seemed
to have evaporated, leaving only a magnificent cope moving
magically before the altar.

As she was describing this, Theo had interrupted to confirm that he too had been to an Armenian mass once, and
experienced exactly the same illusion.

Kirsten continued to describe how the lights in the chapel
had been extinguished, leaving the altar illuminated only by
the flickering light of the candles. The Grand Master had
then turned to the monstrance, removed the golden, silk
covering from it, and raised it high. Everyone knelt and the
Grand Master had chanted three times in his wonderful,
deep voice.

'With this relic of the tunic of our martyred Grand Master,
Jacques de Moulay, we bless you.' He had slowly moved from
side to side, repeating this blessing three times. She concluded it was impressive and the Grand Master obviously

had a charismatic effect. Templars even genuflected when he appeared; the effect was overwhelming.

Charlotte had then asked her whether she had felt anything malign or would she say that these so-called Templars were just a movement with ambitions to make a mark internationally.

Kirsten was silent for a while as she considered that question, until answering, 'There was an afternoon when I had been working on the floor above the library in a room where we were sorting some of the books. This room overlooked the courtyard and I noticed the Indian Templars moving one of the flat burial stones. These stones must be exceedingly heavy, because they needed crowbars and rollers to move it aside. I could see it had covered a stone-lined pit, in the bottom of which I could see a newish-looking coffin. I came to the conclusion that they were preparing the pit for another coffin. I had seen this courtyard before from the room, and Count Alexis had explained that all high-ranking Templars continued to be buried there. However there was something odd about the way the Indians were going about their task; they were giggling and clutching each other in a sort of uncontrolled glee.

'That day I had a lot of manuscripts to collate and was still working when the exit bells started to ring. You will find that you will be issued with metallic tags that are housed in a line at the entrance we use to enter the Castle – you take one on entering and replace it on leaving, so that they know you have left. That evening I ran down and put my tag in its slot. Normally there is a Templar at the entrance, checking one's exit. That evening, no one was there, but when I got to my car I found I had left my purse in the upstairs room so I had to go back to retrieve it; it had my ignition key inside. There was still no one at the entrance, so I left my tag in its slot so as not to alert anyone that I was still in the building. I ran upstairs and picked up my purse but, instead of immediately running out again, I was stopped by the sound of chanting in the courtyard; my curiosity got the better of me and I peered out of the side of the window. The courtyard was full of Templars surrounding three sides of the grave. I could hear the steady beat of drums, which ceased at intervals. In the following silences, I heard the chant of "Bahomet be praised", repeated several times, followed by "Death to his enemies". This drumming and chanting increased in volume. I saw, coming out of the cloister, the Grand Master in a black cope, followed by six Indians bearing a coffin on their shoulders.' Kirsten was obviously distressed at reliving what she had seen; her new friends stared at her intensely. She continued, 'I was overwhelmed with an overpowering sense of – I can't really describe it! Terror, horror and an increasing fear for my own safety. As fast as I could I ran back to my car and drove back to the mundane normality of Zurzach. It had been a nightmare vision.'

Kirsten's recollection drained their ebullience. They tried to analyse her experience.

'Are you sure of the words of their chanting?' asked Nicholas.

Kirsten shook her head. 'The sounds were certainly muffled by the closed windows, but that's how my brain interpreted them. I suppose what frightened me was the sense that this was not a gathering of mourners, but a crowd rejoicing.'

Charlotte exclaimed, 'My God! I hope the occupant of the coffin was not alive!' Afterwards she could give no rational reason for this outburst, and added, 'Sorry Kirsten, but our imaginations have been infected by some questions raised about the Templars before we left London.'

Their dinner party broke up and Theo said he would walk Kirsten back to her hotel and perhaps they could have a calming nightcap there. His gallantry took two hours.

Before reaching the hotel they passed an inn and heard the sound of music and yodelling. They went in and found themselves in the middle of a weekly musical evening – it was entirely genuine and not a tourist performance. While chatting to the innkeeper they discovered he was a jazz enthusiast and Theo suggested that they could provide a jazz quartet as Kirsten had revealed she had brought a guitar with her from America. The innkeeper accepted their offer with alacrity, and once a week this gave them a break from their Templar studies.

11

The next week was without incident, but the experience of Kirsten weighed on their minds. Kirsten had already been allocated a car and another one was allocated to the academics. This saved them being dependent on transport being provided by the Templars. They were told generously that these cars could be used to explore when their day was over. Theo became the constant companion of Kirsten. He explained to the others that this was to help her if she got lost or had a problem with her car. Natural selection continued to thrive.

During the daytime Kirsten was engaged in sorting the books stacked in the floor above the library. When she had sufficient books to return to the library, they were loaded into large laundry baskets and a then, via a lift, trundled to the library. In this transportation she was helped by Theo and Nicholas. The latter was reminded of the film, *Thoroughly Modern Millie*, in which young girls were spirited out of a New York hostel in a drugged condition to disappear into the hands of Chinese white slavers.

Count Alexei had been an intelligent guide to the areas of the library that covered their research. The Count had pointed out to Charlotte an area dealing with the Ark of the Covenant.

He had said, 'When you have established our previous ownership of the Shroud of Turin, you might have time to research the early Templar discovery of the Ark when excavating the Temple Mount in Jerusalem. Some say it was this and not the Holy Grail cup that gave the early Templars their secret spiritual power. I do know, though, that the Grand Master is more interested in proving our ownership of the Shroud.' He then showed her where the relevant documents were kept. He had opened a chest with large drawers in which parchments and other artefacts were stored. Standing behind Charlotte, he began describing these and gently touched her shoulder. 'In addition, we get regular historical treasures from a source I have in Mother Russia. I am due to receive a package, personally delivered next week, from my source, one Ivan Andropov. I shall be away next week, so I wonder if you can help me. We pay him on delivery. I will arrange for our treasurer to have the funds ready and he will expect you to collect them from him when Ivan arrives. Will you do this?'

Charlotte took the opportunity to move away from him and said, 'Of course.'

'You'll find Ivan an eccentric figure, more of a Russian wolf than a bear and usually in need of a good wash.'

Charlotte was not encouraged by the description of the Russian courier, but was happy to conclude her conversation as Count Alexei's hand had been gently stroking the back of her neck. At that moment Nicholas was passing and led her away, saying, 'I found a very interesting thirteenth-century document of interest to us both ... ' When they had moved away he added, 'Don't hesitate to find us if that oily Count gets too fresh.'

Charlotte laughed. 'Thank you.' She kissed him lightly on his lips.

The following week Charlotte was unloading one of the laundry baskets and placing its contents on the library shelves when her work was interrupted by a Templar entering the library with a man looking like an unkempt tramp. He had on a long brown overcoat, threadbare and ragged, a red handkerchief was loosely tied around his neck; he reminded her of an Augustus John picture of a gypsy.

The Templar introduced him as Ivan Andropov and confirmed that he had a package to be handed to her personally on the instructions of Count Alexei. Charlotte felt immediate concern for her visitor; he was deathly white and breathing heavily between bouts of rasping coughs. She gestured for him to sit down, and seeing Kirsten nearby, asked her to give the visitor tea while she went to get the envelope for him from the treasurer.

'*Da! Da!*' he had replied. Around his neck, he had a leather satchel; he swung it from his side and took out a bottle of vodka and immediately took a swig then, wiping his mouth, said, 'I have come from Kiev, walking, hitching lifts and jumping trains. Very boring, very tiring and bad for shoes.'

Kirsten was fascinated to see a dirty red sock emerging from the broken tip of his left shoe.

When Charlotte returned with the envelope, she found Ivan slumped over the library table, his head resting on his arms. He was snoring loudly. Kirsten was keeping an eye on him from a nearby bookcase. She had placed a mug of tea by his side. Charlotte touched his shoulder to wake him. He shot up straight, clasping the package he was to deliver. She handed him the envelope the treasurer had given her. The envelope was sealed with red wax, on which the Grand Master's seal was impressed. Ivan took a deep draught of tea from the mug and held out his hand to take the envelope. Charlotte had a smaller envelope and handed it to him first, explaining it contained a receipt for him to sign.

Ivan nodded. 'First I count, then I sign. Please order car to take me to Zurich. With money I stay the night and return soft class by plane.' He stood up, 'I sit privately.' He took the two envelopes and his package to a nearby table. Charlotte asked Kirsten to arrange the car Ivan had requested. He was a long time counting, but finally returned, dropping the package and the smaller envelope, containing the receipt, in front of Charlotte. He took out the receipt to show he had signed; it was for twenty thousand Swiss francs. He then bowed, picked up his vodka bottle and bowed again. At that moment the Templar who had brought him to the library entered to say that his car was ready to take him to Zurich.

As he left, he said, 'Count Alexei will be pleased with this delivery – priceless papers found hidden in Rasputin's house after his death. Sorry about the wrapping.'

After he had left, Charlotte took the brown paper package and put it in front of her to examine it. It had obviously got wet in transit and was broken at one corner to reveal an under layer of Russian newspapers holding in the contents. She teased up the corner, and as she did so, two silverfish dropped on to the table and scuttled off on to the floor of the library. She turned to Kirsten, who had come back to join her. 'I think we'd better consult the others. Silverfish at large are the last visitors a library needs. Keep an eye out while I get Theo and Nick.'

When the two men joined them they suggested they spread a plastic sheet over the library table, unwrap the package and shake out any remaining silverfish. They stood by with a fly spray which was fortunately nearby. They found a veritable concentration as they sorted the contents on to the table. These were a series of yellowing folders and, within them, faded documents and photographs in old brown envelopes. In addition there was a prayer book covered in calf skin, inscribed with exquisite gold script. From the envelope containing photographs, a woodlouse escaped on to the table.

As they started, Nicholas let out a gasp. He had been delicately turning the pages of the prayer book and suddenly shut it. The others stopped and looked at him. 'Bloody hell! Literally bloody hell! Sick.' He passed it to Theo and muttered, 'Not suitable viewing for the girls.'

Theo opened it slowly and fanned the leaves of the book, and, horrified by some of its illustrations, slammed it shut. He took his hand away as if burnt and whispered, 'Bad Karma'.

At the same time Kirsten had tipped out the contents of the envelope containing the photos; the top ones had faded to a sepia blur, but as they were spread out, their images were clear and Kirsten let out a small cry: 'Oh no, oh no!'

Theo and Nicholas moved beside her. They spread out the photos; they were a series of images of some foul ritual. They featured a stone altar which had a basin-like depression on its top. The altar was like a table and in one of the pictures a veiled, naked woman lay beneath it – a veil covering only her head. Other pictures showed a robed figure holding a knife. The figure's head was grotesquely covered by a goat-like mask. Others showed a baby lying on top of the altar and the menacing figure viewed from the back, holding the dagger high in the air. On the robe the figure was wearing, the number 666 was emblazoned.

The two men looked at each other aghast, Theo exclaiming, 'What on earth … ?'

Nicholas shook his head. 'Could be some appalling Mithraic ritual. One's mind leaps to the conclusion it is not impossible that the priest figure could be Rasputin and, heaven forbid, that the woman involved was the Tsarina.'

Charlotte interrupted, 'For God's sake, let's put everything together again and then decide what to do.'

Feverishly they got the folders, the prayer book and photos together, packed them up in their original wrapping and retied the whole parcel with its dirty string. They pushed their chairs away from the table as if to avoid any contamination from the parcel before deciding what they should do.

'Upon a peak in Darien they looked in wild surmise … ' inappropriately Nicholas quoted.

Kirsten leant forward and whispered, 'Let's get out of here with this filth and burn it in those woods outside Zurzach where we walk.'

At that moment the door of the library opened and the Templar treasurer entered.

'I'm leaving my office early today and Count Alexei instructed me to collect the package you have just received and put it in our safe. The Russian messenger got a large sum for it. Difficult to believe papers can be that valuable.' He turned to Charlotte. 'Have you got the signed receipt?'

The small envelope was still on the table and Charlotte handed it over and pointed to the package. The treasurer picked it up and left without saying another word.

They sat around the empty table trying to make sense of what they had just seen. Nicholas said, 'Let's get back to the hotel and after baths to cleanse ourselves, meet for drinks to analyse the meaning of it all.'

It was a subdued group that sat on the hotel terrace where they had moved so that they could talk without being overheard. At first they sat in silence as they finished their drinks.

Theo started the discussion. 'What in the name of heaven is really going on? The picture painted by Colonel Baker is of a cult with a political agenda. At first it appeared to be an eccentric organisation revolving around a charismatic figure; to me it seemed basically harmless and, with its close links to American fundamentalists, mostly ludicrous.'

Nicholas nodded. 'Yes, but I found the Teutonic Knights coming on the scene a sinister development.'

Kirsten chipped in. 'Well, I find that I am quite spooked, having seen the Templars' preparations for that burial in the courtyard. What if, behind it all, they are feeding on some really dark beliefs and practices? The package today, for which they have paid so much money, might be associated with such evil within the organisation.'

Charlotte shook her head in bewilderment. 'Why don't we question Count Alexei and see his reaction, saying the package had burst open?'

Kirsten shook her head. 'You don't really think he would

acknowledge this package as destined for the Grand Master. Surely he would just express suitable shock and say that the Russian was delivering it merely for historical investigation. Then he would be under no obligation to tell us anything. Anyway in ten days we will be gone – and I say thank God! Have you three discovered anything fundamentally important in the areas you were asked to investigate?'

They all shook their heads. They had found no hard historical facts backed up by documentary evidence. Everything was hearsay and with every century after the Dissolution of the Templars the stories got more colourful.

Nicholas elaborated. 'If you accepted that the Templars had become corrupted by Gnostic beliefs, worshipped idols and practised exotic rituals, then Philip the Fair of France had good reason to obliterate the Order. Whatever the rumours spread, it is highly unlikely they had all the relics attributed to them: the Ark of the Covenant, the Shroud of Turin or the Holy Grail cup. Of course some claim these would have been kept secret, only to be displayed at selected times.'

Charlotte joined in. 'When Philip the Fair involved the Inquisition, the Templars had been tortured to admit to sacrilegious acts and worshipping an androgynous head of an idol named Bahomet. The fact that Kirsten thought she heard this name being chanted adds to the nightmare, but in reality the judgement of history is that only a tiny minority were guilty, and then probably only of unnatural vice. They were obliterated so that their wealth could be pinched by the French King; the Pope frustrated him by getting a large portion of the wealth transferred to the Knights of Malta.'

Theo nodded in agreement. 'Their secrecy was to blame, encouraging rumours. As far as I can see none of our research so far is going to bolster our hosts' fantasies – unless we are brainwashed like nutty Professor Jones.' Later, they would remember this remark.

12

Next afternoon, Charlotte was in the library sorting through a pile of parchments, stored in a long drawer. She was interrupted in her work by Count Alexei arriving in the company of the woman who had been with the Grand Master at the Zurich symposium. Count Alexei introduced Lady Natasha, saying that she had come to invite Charlotte to join the Grand Master, who was free that morning, and wished to discuss the results of her research.

Charlotte's first impression was of an overwhelming scent of a heavy, musky perfume. The woman's dark hair was still cut like a boy's and there was something androgynous about her. She was wearing a dark grey, tailored dress and high-heeled boots. The only indication of her membership of the Templar Order was a gold medallion around her neck engraved with the Templar insignia.

Lady Natasha took Charlotte by the right arm without the formality of shaking her hand. 'I am sorry to interrupt you, but the Grand Master is going away tomorrow and would like to hear how you are progressing before he leaves.'

Charlotte was annoyed by this sudden invitation. She had slept badly the night before, troubled by the revelations in the Russian package. She had woken late and had only had time to seize a coffee and a croissant before joining Nicholas who was waiting in their car to drive them to the Castle. In her rush she had failed to take her daily hypnosis antidote pill and had brought it with her in the car. It was still there in the glove compartment. Fortunately Nicholas was at the end of the library and Charlotte explained to Lady Natasha that she needed to have a quick word with him. She told

Nicholas of her need to have the car keys urgently; how she had been summoned to see the Grand Master and had remembered she had not taken her antidote pill that morning, which was still in the glove compartment of the car. She then returned to Lady Natasha, explaining that she needed to go to the car to collect a clean shirt.

Natasha smiled sweetly and said, 'I'll come with you. There is a cloakroom I can show you near the Grand Master's office where you can change.'

When they got to the Castle door by the car park, Lady Natasha was fortunately distracted by the arrival of one of the New Teutonic Knights, who engaged her in conversation. Charlotte was therefore able not only to find her clean shirt, but also to take one of the pills. She remembered that the War Office doctor had told them they took an hour before they had any effect. As she locked the car, Lady Natasha was hurrying towards her.

'We must not delay; the Grand Master does not tolerate lateness. Forget about changing; you're fine. I'll look after your shirt.' She snatched it out of Charlotte's hand and, beckoning her to follow, walked swiftly down the long corridors. They passed the entrance to the Templar chapel and walked on until they reached an imposing set of double doors. They went through these into a large reception area. Just inside the door there was a large mahogany desk and, in the rest of the room, two large leather-covered sofas in front of an elaborately carved stone fireplace in which two large logs smouldered gently. Over the fireplace hung a life-size portrait of the Grand Master giving a blessing.

Lady Natasha gestured towards the sofas. 'Wait there – the GM's PA must be in his office. I just need a word with him and then Sergeant Maggie will give you tea or coffee.'

Lady Natasha went to a door on the other side of the room and punched in a code. There was an audible click, and pushing the door, Lady Natasha opened it, but for a moment stood staring into the room. Charlotte heard the raised voice of the Grand Master.

'How dare you! You know you must ring first. My business with Maggie is not yet finished.'

Charlotte was startled by the venom in Natasha's reply.

'I can see – your business – indeed!'

The door was slammed as Natasha moved inside. Charlotte heard the sound of raised voices. A few minutes passed, the inner door opened and Sergeant Maggie was pushed through, the door immediately slammed shut; Maggie was flushed and breathing heavily, one side of her face bore a reddening weal, her shirt was partly unbuttoned.

'Sorry, I'm Sergeant Maggie – one of the Grand Master's PA's.' She turned away to button her shirt; she realised the absurdity of the situation. 'Excuse me, I made a stupid mistake by buttoning my shirt wrongly this morning – the Grand Master was furious with me, and I was just putting it right, you see, when his stuck-up … ' Maggie muttered a Swiss expletive … 'Anyway she burst in and so I'm in double trouble now.' She dabbed her eyes. 'Can I get you a coffee while you wait?' She disappeared into an alcove at the side of the room without waiting for an answer. Muffled sobbing accompanied the sound of a kettle coming to the boil.

In the office beyond the closed door, Lady Natasha was arched back over the Grand Master's table. At first there was only silence beyond the office door – silence which was eventually broken by faint cries, both male and female. In her innocence Charlotte presumed they were exchanging angry blows and she sat transfixed by what seemed to be a developing American-style TV drama. A further ten minutes passed before the door was opened by the Grand Master. Charlotte had been given coffee and a French *Vogue* to read, while Maggie had disappeared back into the alcove.

The Grand Master appeared totally calm. 'I am so sorry for the delay. Do come in. Natasha is very interested in the

Shroud of Turin so I hope you don't mind her sitting in while we discuss the results of your research.'

Natasha had moved to a nearby easy chair, leaving a chair in front of the table dominating the room. This room was decorated with dove-grey walls and plain matching curtains. Beyond the table were large French windows opening on to a balcony, overlooking the inner courtyard. The Grand Master used this balcony to make solemn pronouncements to the Templars. On one side of the room were two doors; one led to a bathroom and one to a dressing room.

When Charlotte was seated, the Grand Master leant forward, putting his elbows on the table and joining his fingers together. He smiled warmly at her.

'Well now, Charlotte, what are your conclusions about our historical ownership of the Shroud?' His demeanour was so charming and his smile so warm that Charlotte found it hard to believe that he could be some diabolical agent. Surely he was unaware of the Russian package, probably sent because of some Templar references; maybe after all it was just a harmless cult with genuine concerns for the safety of Christian pilgrims to Jerusalem. Charlotte sat silently for a moment, transfixed by the brilliance of his blue eyes. She dismissed Nicholas's comment that when he had shaken the Grand Master's hand he had been reminded of the tales of the hypnotic use Hitler made of similar blue eyes, fixing those in front of him with a silent stare. The stare of the Grand Master was beautiful at that moment; she leant back in her chair and her fear left her.

The Grand Master broke her silence. 'Don't be shy or afraid to reveal your conclusions. We know that in 1988, when the Shroud was examined by those teams of scientists, they concluded it was only one thousand years old: a medieval forgery, though one of which they could not explain the technique used in its production.' He paused, opened a drawer in his table and took out some papers. Looking at

91

them he continued, 'But now we have another scientist, Dr Raymond Rogers, who had examined the Shroud in 1978 and had also declared it a forgery. He said then, "I don't believe in miracles that defy the laws of nature." ' The Grand Master smiled. 'Silly saying that, because defying the laws of nature defines a miracle. However in 2005 he changed his mind when it was admitted that the postage-size fragments of the Shroud that were given to the scientists in 1988 came from a piece woven into the Shroud to repair fire damage a thousand years ago. The pieces they examined were found to contain cotton fibres, whereas the Shroud is made of linen – what a crazy scientific examination! Anyway, this Dr Rogers made a video in 2005 after this mistake was made known. In it he states that the Shroud was probably the one used to bury the body of Christ. So the Shroud we owned was genuine. When Philip the Fair destroyed us, we were forced to sell it, but are preparing a case to have it returned to us from Turin. Now then, what are your conclusions after examining our archives?'

Charlotte sat up straight before answering. 'The Catholic Church has no official position on the Shroud. I have mixed feelings – I am open-minded. When the 1988 conclusions were announced by the scientists, one part of me was glad; you see I feel absolute proof that it really was the original Shroud almost forced us to believe in the Resurrection of Christ, removing the blessing he gave to those who believed without seeing him after his Resurrection appearances. From the start, when you invited me to research your claim, I have been puzzled as to why you need to have it proven.'

The Grand Master sat back in his chair, his face expressing amazement. A snort of derision came from his mistress, Lady Natasha.

'My dear girl, we were forced to sell it after the suppression of our Order. The Shroud is ours. Just as Jews were forced to sell their pictures at derisory prices to the Nazis and are now having them returned to them, likewise the Shroud should be returned to us.'

Charlotte considered the comparison absurd. 'Well, the Jews can prove past ownership and having their possessions stolen is recent history. Your claim is obscure, particularly because the Shroud was lost to history during the time you claim it was yours. You have also to prove you really are survivors of the original Order. Anyway, if you had it in the past, what use did you make of it and what use would you put it to now?'

The Grand Master's eyes narrowed; his face flushed with anger. As he began to answer her, he punctuated each sentence by slapping the table with his right hand.

'Stupid girl! When we first owned it, it was kept secretly within the Order. It was one of our main sources of spiritual power and representations of it were distributed throughout our territories. For instance, you may recall in a property in your country in Somerset which had been a Templar property, a representation of the face of Christ has been revealed during redecoration, a face similar to that on the Shroud. It seems Count Alexei, who gave you a large amount of information from our archives, failed to lead you to the right conclusions.'

Charlotte was not cowed by his anger. 'Of course I read all the material exhaustively here and during my years at Cambridge. I am afraid my conclusions are that there is no concrete proof, only hearsay, repetition of claims, but no documentary proof. Nor have you answered my question: what would you do with it if you had it given you by the Church, because of your flimsy claim?'

The Grand Master's face clouded again; he slammed the table hard with both hands. 'How dare you call it a flimsy claim! You are an ignoramus. Of course our claims are proof enough. As to your impertinent question as to what we would do with it – in these days of unbelief we would display it permanently to succour the faithful, and convert unbelievers to the truth of the Resurrection – especially the infidel Muslims. It would not be locked away in Turin Cathedral, appearing infrequently. Already we have a site near the Holy Sepulchre in Jerusalem and permission to build a magnificent round Templar Church, where the Shroud would be permanently on display. Unfortunately you appear to be obstinately blinkered. I suggest you go back to Count Alexei and get his help. We intended to give you all a bonus, twice the amount of your pre-payment, if your conclusions helped us. We are preparing a case to take to the International Court at The Hague.' He stood up, came round to Charlotte and put a hand on her shoulder. 'Look at me; I want you to realise the value of our great cause. Because of this, I will now reveal to you overwhelming proof. I have here, in the drawer of this table, the original deed of sale by the Charney family to the House of Savoy at the beginning of the fourteenth century. You will remember Geoffrey de Charney was burnt with the Grand Master, Jacques de Moulay. Come, we will examine it together.'

Charlotte was startled by this revelation. It would certainly be a highlight of her career as a historian to be one of the first witnesses if the deeds were genuine. However she was sceptical, wondering why they had not revealed this before.

The Grand Master told her to bring her chair round to his side of the table. He turned to Natasha and asked her to bring the necessary white gloves so that Charlotte could handle the deed.

Charlotte moved round to sit beside him. He opened a further drawer in the table. Inside were a red document case and a pair of white gloves, which he put on. Natasha appeared with a pair for Charlotte, sealed in plastic.

The Grand Master explained that the gloves were treated to avoid contaminating the deed.

Charlotte put on her gloves. She was surprised that they

felt slightly damp. The document case was opened, revealing a rolled parchment. The Grand Master took it out and placed it on the table. He held its lower edge, while Lady Natasha came to the other side of the table and unrolled it. It was about three feet long. It appeared to be an exquisite medieval manuscript. Its lettering was gold and red. At its top was a large coat of arms.

'Let us stand together to examine it.' The Grand Master put his arm around Charlotte's shoulder, and drew her to him. 'See the coat of arms at the top is of the House of Savoy, and the wax seals at the end are those of that royal house and of the Charney family who bought the Shroud from the Templars. See also the date.'

Unfortunately Charlotte's vision was slowly becoming blurred; she felt sick and had to sit down. Slowly she slumped forward, her head resting on the table. Natasha released her hold on the parchment and it sprang back into a roll. The Grand Master took Charlotte's wrist and felt her pulse. He put his thumb up to signify to Natasha that the impregnated gloves had done their work. He went through to the reception and asked Maggie to help them carry Charlotte to the bed in the dressing room. When she was laid there, Natasha loosened Charlotte's clothing and removed her tights. Natasha dismissed Maggie and then moved over to the Grand Master and kissed him.

'Work your magic, my lord, but don't give her one of your blessings at the end.'

The Grand Master looked sulky. 'She is quite beautiful, with lovely skin. She looks so young and almost virginal.'

Natasha laughed softly. 'She is – I've just checked. We don't want a scandal on our hands. I'll be next door; don't waste time, we usually only have an hour.'

The Grand Master moved a chair to the head of the bed and leant over Charlotte. 'Can you hear me, Charlotte?'

She sighed in reply before softly replying, 'Yes.'

He took her hand. 'You and I have just had the privilege of examining the historic proof of the sale by the Templars of the Holy Shroud of Turin to the Charney family and then to the House of Savoy at the beginning of the fourteenth century. We have verified the seals together, Charlotte. You are one of the first to see this proof of our past possession of the Shroud. You now believe that it belonged to the Templars, don't you, Charlotte?' He squeezed Charlotte's hand.

'Yes, I believe.'

The Grand Master patted her hand. 'As you are leaving soon, it would make me happy if you would sign a statement that you have seen the deed and that it is overwhelming proof of our previous possession. If you do this you will be awarded the bonus I spoke of.' Charlotte stirred uneasily, which surprised him. He squeezed her hand again. 'Will you sign the statement?'

Charlotte started moving her head from side to side, but eventually murmured, 'Yes, I will sign.'

The Grand Master let go of her hand and left the dressing room to collect the statement, which Sergeant Maggie had already typed and given to Lady Natasha, who was waiting in his office. Together they went back into the dressing room and to their astonishment they found Charlotte sitting up, her expression one of alarm. An hour had elapsed since she had taken the antidote pill and it had now taken effect, but she had no recollection of what had happened since putting on the white gloves. She had a massive headache and, feeling dizzy, she sank back into the bed, groaning, 'What's happened – where am I?'

Before they could answer, Sergeant Maggie appeared and told them that an angry Nicholas was in the reception area, demanding to speak to Charlotte. He had begun to be seriously concerned at her prolonged absence. His arrival could not have been more inopportune. Maggie was sent to assure him that Charlotte would soon be ready to leave and meanwhile, she was told to give him some refreshment. While Nicholas had been in the reception area alone, he had strolled around the room and noticed that on the desk Maggie had been sorting several sizes of the Grand Master's notepaper. He leant over the desk, took two embossed envelopes and four sheets of paper and quickly folded them before tucking them into the inside pocket of his jacket. He then picked up a magazine and was sitting innocently reading it when Sergeant Maggie reappeared.

The Templar drug had also a prepared medicine to mitigate the after-effects and Natasha proceeded to give this to Charlotte, still in her semi-drugged condition. A quarter of an hour later Natasha helped her to get up, though she was still ashen-faced.

Natasha said that Nicholas had come to collect her and that she must go back with him to rest at their hotel. They would arrange for their accredited doctor to visit her at six-thirty that evening. She had continued to say that unfortunately as they were a registered organisation, Swiss health regulations meant she had to sign an agreement to say she was fit enough to leave them. Natasha had folded the statement that had been prepared confirming Charlotte's verification of the historical proof she had recently witnessed so that only the ending was displayed. It read, 'Signed by Charlotte Fox' and then, underneath, it was witnessed by Sergeant Maggie and Natasha.

Charlotte swayed as she moved, saying, 'I'm afraid my vision's all wonky.'

Natasha knew this would be the case and took her hand and guided it to the signature area, telling her not to worry and sign as best she could. She led her out of the room and told Nicholas to take her back to the hotel and put her to bed. They were sending a doctor later but assumed Charlotte probably had some bug or the onset of a severe monthly disability and hoped she would feel better later.

13

Before dinner the doctor had come to the hotel to see Charlotte and apart from giving her a tonic, said that she had no further problems healthwise. After his visit she joined the others on the hotel terrace and it was obvious to them all that Charlotte must have been drugged in some way during her time with the Grand Master. Try as she might, she could only remember up to the time of putting on the gloves to examine the parchment; the rest of her memory was blank until Nicholas collected her. They agreed that after dinner, Nicholas and Theo should take their secure mobile phones given to them by Colonel Baker, and drive a little way outside Zurzach to contact him. They were surprised that when they switched on their phones, they had each received a message from Colonel Baker sent one hour earlier. 'Cat's-Eyes one here – ring me immediately.'

Theo nudged Nicholas to give him the task. He was instantly answered by Colonel Baker barking, 'Do you check the Templar website every day?'

Nick gave a startled, 'No ... '

Colonel Baker was obviously seething with anger. 'Well you bloody well should! Are you taking your daily antidotes, because it seems not, particularly Miss Eggs twenty-five?'

It was a warm night. Nicholas broke into a sweat.

'What do you mean?'

There was a pause, then Colonel Baker continued speaking slowly and deliberately, as if to a class of dim children. 'What I mean is that either our antidote does not work, or Miss Eggs twenty-five has lost her marbles. There is a long announcement on the Templar website saying that a well-known Cambridge historian, Charlotte Fox, has discovered a document proving conclusively that the Templars had possession of the Shroud and sold it to the Charney family under economic pressure and then it was bought by the House of Savoy. This evidence would play a major part in the Templar case being prepared for the international court in The Hague to gain reownership of the Shroud. What the hell's been going on?'

Nicholas explained the happenings of the day and assured the Colonel that they had just driven to find a safe spot to report to him, in case their hotel was bugged. He agreed the Colonel's news was shattering and told him they had no prior knowledge of the information he had just given them.

The Colonel was silent for a moment. 'I'm alarmed Miss Eggs twenty-five had no recollection of her meeting – I'll have to consult our medical team. Meanwhile, you've only a few days left – you'll have to find out more. It's no good spending your time farting around in their library; you've got to look further afield. What has happened today is ominous. I want results, but watch your backs.'

He was to get more results than anyone could have imagined.

When Theo and Nicholas returned to their hotel, they went again to the terrace and ordered large drinks. They agreed it would not help to tell Charlotte about the website announcement but hoped that the next day her memory might return to give them a clue as to how she had been drugged. The immediate problem was to think of some way that they could find out more about any hidden secrets of a damning nature about the Templars of Zurzach. They had very little contact with the members apart from Count Alexei. They considered getting him drunk, but concluded from their observations of him that he had an extremely high alcoholic tolerance.

Theo moved into an American-style solution and proposed that if he could be made very drunk, then perhaps they could get him to one of their rooms and threaten him with something simple, like water-boarding, or perhaps castration! Its absurdity was obvious as soon as he said it and both Nicholas and he laughed at the possibility, as the hotel rooms were not well insulated for sound. Nicholas added dryly, that because of this, the cries of the Count would be heard by all their neighbours, and no doubt they would be besieged by people wanting to know which channel their TV was tuned in to. The hotel barman had told them that the majority of the guests were geriatric, and apart from floating in the hot spring pools, spent their time watching adult films on their TVs.

They then considered seeing if they could break into any Templar offices in the castle, but to get in at night after the seven o'clock curfew would be impossible. Next they wondered whether Colonel Baker could send an IT expert to hack into the Grand Master's computer system, but then realised that he only had handwritten correspondence and that the details of his running of the Templars were probably all in his brain. In the end they concluded that the only area which might reveal something of interest, was the chapel, which might contain evidence relating to depraved rituals. Unfortunately it appeared permanently locked during the day, but they agreed that they would take turns to find out if at any time it was open, as they were close by in the library most of the time.

The following day they were given the opportunity they sought.

Every quarter of an hour one of them had peered out of the library door and, if the coast was clear, walked to the chapel to see if they could get in. Theo was about to leave the library to do this when he saw the chapel doors burst open; a cleaning woman wearing a scruffy smock ran out, the smock incongruously embossed with the red cross of the Templars. She was closely followed by Sergeant Maggie waving a broom; they sped down the corridor shouting Italian imprecations. Theo could see the chapel door had been left ajar, so he summoned Nicholas and together they hurried inside and shut the door. The interior was austere with plain stone walls. In the Templar fashion, it was round with massive stone pillars supporting its roof, which tapered over the pillars to its outside walls. Against these, were a series of small chapels, which in a Catholic era would have been used as daily mass chapels. Its appearance in the present day was almost Calvinistic; the Norman structure was devoid of internal decoration, save for some tapestries, the side chapels were without altars and the main altar in the church adorned solely with a book. They went straight to this book in the hope that it might reveal secrets, but it was a modern Bible, printed in German and English. The only curious feature was that it was open at the final page of Chapter 13 of the book of Revelation, whose ending is, 'Let those who have insight, calculate the number of the beast, for it is the number of a man. That number is 666.'

The chapel tapestries depicted Templar castles and battles, one of which was swaying out from the wall, as if in a draught. They looked behind it and saw a slightly open door, seemingly controlled by an electronic entry panel at its side. The door revealed a spiral staircase leading downwards; as they concluded it might be leading to a crypt below, they hoped it might reveal matters of more significance.

The spiral staircase seemed unending. Theo counted the steps on the way down and calculated there were more than a hundred of them by the time they reached the floor of the crypt; they reckoned they must be under ground level as halfway down the light from small slit windows had ceased. They then came to a large thickened glass window looking into the waters of the moat. Nicholas could see a large carp on the other side, moving slowly with its mouth open, and he was incongruously reminded of his college Master, Canon

Frobisher. A faint light from below illuminated the last part of the staircase. As they reached the floor of the crypt they saw that this light came from a multitude of red sanctuary lamps, illuminating a series of side chapels. Adjusting their eyes to the dim light, they were stunned by what they saw. A round crypt, which was as big as the chapel above, had in the middle a large stone altar. It was similar to the one illustrated in the Russian prayer book, the one that Charlotte had taken from the messenger for Count Alexei. The altar was at least ten feet long and six feet wide. A large brown glass sanctuary lamp above the altar illuminated a deep depression in its surface. Its huge stone slab rested on six black marble columns. Beneath it was placed a four foot-wide-mattress, covered in some red sheeting.

Together they moved forward to examine it. Silently they pointed to the inside of the depression on top of the altar with a hole for draining. This basin was stained dark brown on its base with what looked like more recent stains on its sides of a reddish hue.

'A Mithraic altar if ever there was one,' whispered Nicholas.

Theo stepped back quickly, making an orthodox sign of the cross.

The chapel had an overwhelming perfume of musky incense, scent similar to that worn by Lady Natasha when visiting them in the library.

They moved to examine the smaller chapels within the outer walls – mirroring the mass chapels in the church above. The largest had walls covered in black silk, dimly illuminated by three grey sanctuary lamps. It had a black marble altar, on which rested a black coffin with two solid iron candlesticks holding black candles. In a niche behind the altar stood a life-sized statue, robed in red, except for its face which was covered by a black veil under its hood. The veil was embroidered in gold leaf with the figures '666'.

Nicholas and Theo were oppressed by the menace of the

whole place, though later it could be viewed as an absurdity in the cold light of a twenty-first-century day. They moved around the vast space, pausing for only a short time in the other chapels. One was dedicated to the martyred fourteenth-century Grand Master, Jacques de Moulay; behind its altar was a graphic painting of his burning alive before Notre Dame. One dedicated to the Teutonic Knights was absurd in its garishness: its red walls were decorated with swastikas and SS dagger signs. Most outrageously its altar had behind it the famous painting of Hitler in silver armour, riding on a horse, holding aloft a flag. Finally they stood in amazement at another chapel dedicated to the Indian goddess Kali, the Goddess of Destruction. Its altar contained a stone figure of the goddess, and on a side wall was a photograph of one of the Templar Indians strangling the Arab assassin – the same as in the Dolder Grand Hotel attack. Etched on the altar in gold lettering was the inscription 'Ave Thuggee'.

Nicholas gasped, 'So the Indians here are Thugs. Whatever next! Let's get out of here quick.'

The small chapels covered most of the outer wall space in the crypt, but a small area was approached through an arch. In this area were two lines of cupboards, and between them was a door. They looked in the cupboards, which contained black silk robes and shelving displaying frightening masks, some of cats, some of goat-like heads. They then opened the door between the cupboards, revealing a changing area with cubicles and showers and lavatories, utterly plain and a reminder of a saner, cleaner, modern world.

What they had seen exceeded their wildest imagination and was sufficient to reveal the real driving force of this pseudo-Templar cult. Having seen more than enough, they moved quickly towards the spiral staircase, but their exit was frustrated.

First they heard cries from above and a woman screaming obscenities, and as the sound got louder, they could also hear the distinct sounds of the Indians chattering excitedly. Nicholas and Theo turned back and instinctively darted towards the two cupboards, taking one each, hiding amongst the silk robes and closing the sliding doors. They could hear the sound of people sliding and slithering down the stairs, ending with a heavy thud on the crypt floor and a girl crying out, 'No, no!' An Indian voice shouted, 'Put her out now, she's too strong – we can't have her damaging the coffin.'

A horrible gurgling followed, then the Indian voice again. 'Oh Kali, what a fat slob we've got here. One, two, three – lift.' There was the sound of the Indians giggling. There was a pause, and they heard the coffin being opened on the altar, then grunting as the body was lifted again, and a final thud as it was dumped in the coffin. Another pause, then the sound of the rattle of metal. Again an Indian voice: 'There, she's manacled in now. Lady Natasha should find this to her liking.' There was more laughter and they then heard the sound of the Indians climbing the staircase and the door closing above.

Nicholas and Theo shot out of their cupboards.

'What next, Nick? We're in deadly shit here.'

Nicholas whispered, 'I agree. I nearly sneezed in my cupboard – the robes reek – let's go. When we get into the chapel above, we can hide behind those massive pillars until we are sure the coast is clear, but we can't leave the girl.' Saying this, they went over to the coffin. The lid was off, lying by the side of the altar. Inside, lying unconscious, was Sergeant Maggie, her hands and feet held by manacles.

Theo said, 'Let's hope she comes round soon. It'll be impossible if she doesn't, but if we can get her upstairs, we can use one of the laundry baskets from the library and get her away in one of our cars. OK? Come on. Let's skedaddle.'

He spoke too soon.

The door at the top of the staircase clicked open and they

could hear a man and a woman talking; sound travelled down the stairs as if funnelled by a vertical ear trumpet. Nicholas and Theo rushed back into their cupboards. Lady Natasha and Karl, the deputy Grand Master, entered the crypt. Lady Natasha went over to the coffin.

'She's still unconscious – Sergeant Assad said she would come round in about half an hour; they certainly have perfected their Thuggee craft since we first discovered them – a great asset to have in house! I'll come back later to have my fun with the slut. Anyway, Karl, you said that you wanted a chat with me where we will not be overheard. Let's go to one of those benches by the vestment cupboards.'

Neither Nicholas nor Theo could hear this exchange on the other side of the crypt; it was a great shock to them both to hear the benches being moved near the cupboards so that the two Templars could sit back more comfortably. They settled opposite the cupboard in which Nicholas was hiding.

Karl said, 'Are you sure the GM will agree to Maggie facing the ultimate sanction of burial alive? You really do seem to have it in for her. We have to be very careful when it's one of us; I mean relations eventually need to know.'

Natasha laughed. 'Don't worry, she's an orphan and after a suitable period we will report her disappearance to the authorities. Anyway it's good for discipline in the Order; it's a long time since a Templar was so foolish, and it's salutary for the newly sworn Templars to see the reality.'

Karl interrupted. 'I know that, but surely the lesser sentence of a major flogging would be sufficient in this case.'

Natasha's voice filled with anger. 'You don't understand. She's got a major crush on the Grand Master and unfortunately it appears it's beginning to be reciprocated. I will not tolerate this undermining of the hierarchical structure of the Order. I had it out with the GM yesterday and he agreed she will have to go, but we needed a good reason. Today I found it, in that half an hour ago I found she had left the chapel door open after a row with one of the postulant Italians who was cleaning. When I berated Maggie about this, she swiped at my face with a wet mop, publicly mocking my authority.'

Nicholas was stunned by this casual discussion of burying someone alive. It highlighted their own danger.

Natasha continued relentlessly, 'I could have ordered Sergeant Assad to have despatched her there and then.'

Karl nodded. 'Well, I suppose we shall have to have a brief court martial when the GM returns later today – so be it.'

Natasha smiled sweetly. 'So be it; so it will be! Now, Karl, tell me the result of the council meeting of national Masters. Have our Jerusalem plans been finalised?'

Karl stood up. 'Do you mind if I stretch my legs? I feel a twinge of cramp coming on and also I need a leak.'

'Of course, my darling, not prostate trouble I hope.' Natasha gave an unpleasant snigger.

When Karl returned, they began slowly walking to and fro in front of the cupboards. Until then, Theo had only heard the murmur of their voices in his position in the other cupboard; in fact he had nearly dozed off. The noise of them opposite his own cupboard woke him up, which was fortunate as he was a heavy snorer and if he had been discovered because of this, it would have been a farcical dénouement. The two Templars chose to sit again, but on the bench near his cupboard.

Karl began speaking. 'I think you know we've shelved the idea of attacking Turin Cathedral, disguised as Arabs, to seize the Shroud. Some of us might have been captured and our cover blown.'

Natasha laughed. 'Thank Bahomet for that. I thought it a crazy idea. Anyway that girl, the young Cambridge don doing research for us, has, with a little help, confirmed our previous ownership of the Shroud, which will strengthen our case at The Hague court. We announced it last night on our website.'

'Good heavens,' Karl exclaimed, 'that's great news. Anyway, Jerusalem it is and the bombing of the mosque on Temple Mount. It will certainly ignite an Israeli–Islamic conflagration and our intelligence says that the UN will move in to control the whole area. This of course will put us centre stage.' Natasha clapped her hands. Karl continued, 'We have an under-cover Templar passing himself off as a genuine Jew, who works as a pilot with one of the local Israeli helicopter teams. As you know, the great day has been arranged and he will take a helicopter up for testing, and then land at a spot near the Shaar Zion.' Theo did not hear clearly the name of the landing site as he was pinching his nose to stop himself sneezing, but he heard the continuation.

'At four o'clock precisely three of our crack commando boys will be there, disguised as Armenian priests; two of them will have machine guns hidden under their robes and the third the bomb. They are already in Jerusalem. They will come out of the gate and board the helicopter. Underneath their disguise they will be dressed as Israeli soldiers so that Israel will be blamed for the bombing.'

Natasha clapped her hands again. 'Wonderful! Karl, that's great, but why are you looking miserable?' Karl sat silently. Natasha moved close to him. 'What's the trouble, darling?'

He replied, 'You! I love you, you see.'

Natasha looked around, fearing that this statement might be overheard.

'Sh! You know I'm utterly committed to GM even if I have to share him with others.' She pressed a hand on his thigh. 'But you know I love you as well, I lust for you; next time the GM goes on his travels,' she paused for a moment, ' … why not?' She left the question hanging in the air.

Theo, hearing this exchange, inwardly writhed, thinking they were depraved, all of them, though his overwhelming horror was at what he had heard about the planned atrocity in Jerusalem.

Natasha continued, 'To ensure success we shall be performing here the great ritual, enhanced by additions gleaned from our recently acquired Rasputin book.'

Karl interrupted. 'I'm afraid this is what is really worrying me to the point of despair. Our usual monthly grand rituals using bull calves seem to give us the essential powers we seek, but this new Russian ritual is moving on to a different spiritual plane, involving the sacrifice of a baby. Our young Regan produced that baby a month ago. What nobody knows, apart from her, is that I am the father. The GM has promised her she will join our inner circle if she surrenders the baby. This promise comes not only with money, but also access to the Elixir of Youth that we take monthly. I am deeply uneasy, nature overcoming my Templar convictions. I also think the council should have been consulted first. Do we know this heightened ritual will guarantee the success we seek?'

Natasha was temporarily startled but moved closer to Karl. 'Of course I understand, my darling, but now I absolutely promise we'll play at making babies every time GM is on his travels. Now let's go and have a drinky or two, then I'll come back to have a little fun with our slut in the coffin. I shall enjoy putting the lid on the top,' she began to snigger, 'putting the lid on her for ever.'

Nicholas and Theo heard their laughter growing less and less as they left the crypt until it stopped after a click of the door at the top of the staircase. They left their hiding places. They did not know which item of overheard conversation they should tackle first; neither had heard every word except when the two Templars had been talking in front of their respective cupboards, but each had grasped the terrible fate planned for the girl in the coffin and both had heard the threat to the Jerusalem mosque. They had a whispered consultation, but agreed that if both threats were to be foiled, they must themselves be sure of escaping. They were just moving towards the spiral staircase when they heard the door above open again and the excited voices of the Indians. Theo and Nicholas fled back to their hiding places.

The Indians entered the crypt and went straight to the coffin. One of them said, 'She should be fully conscious in ten minutes, but we'd better make sure and give her a stimulant injection – that Lady Natasha is a real devil.' The Indians giggled again, but this sound was lost as the girl within the coffin began to groan and rattled the chains securing her hands and feet. One of the Indians said, 'OK. We can report that the little piggy here is ripe for treatment now; the burial's scheduled for eight this evening.'

This chilling exchange faded as they left the crypt and ascended the stairs again.

Nicholas and Theo left their cupboards. Nicholas spoke first. 'This is becoming a nightmare farce, popping in and out of our cupboards like cuckoo-clock figures. Do we leg it and try and take the girl with us now, or hide her first and come back when the others can keep a watch?'

Sergeant Maggie heard them and began to scream and rattle her chains. The two men ran to the coffin; the girl stopped screaming and looked at them in astonishment. They began to undo the clamps around her hands and feet; they were fixed with butterfly screws. They assured her they were going to rescue her, but first she must lie quietly in her coffin, and as soon as she heard Lady Natasha enter the crypt again, she was to scream loudly and cause a distraction. They were unsure how to deal with her tormentor until they spotted the squat black candlesticks by the coffin. Deciding they could be effective instruments and picking them up, they hid behind the altar.

They heard footsteps descending the stairs; Maggie began to scream, the footsteps quickened and Natasha walked quickly to the coffin, her high heels clicking precisely like a metronome on the stone floor.

She reached the coffin and snarled, 'Stop that at once.'

Maggie continued to scream so that Natasha shouted: 'Stop that you … ' Her sentence was not completed. Felled by a blow from Theo, she collapsed like a house of cards. She never saw him, nor what hit her.

Nicholas and Theo moved with speed, fuelled by the rush of adrenalin. With difficulty they lifted Maggie out of the coffin and replaced her with the unconscious Lady Natasha. Already blood was oozing from the wound inflicted by the candlestick. The two men did not exchange a word as they fixed the manacles on Natasha's wrists and ankles; they then lifted the coffin lid, which was resting by the side of the altar. They saw the coffin had holes in its side to allow air to circulate within, so that rather than suffocate, its occupant could still be conscious at the time of burial. They secured the lid firmly with the large brass butterfly screws on the side of the coffin.

Theo wiped his hands on the sides of his trousers. 'That will keep her out of the way until we're gone from this hell hole. We'll ring them, or get Colonel Baker to tell them where this Natasha bitch has gone – but only when we're well on our way.'

They helped Maggie to hide in one of the cupboards; Nicholas explained that they would rescue her via one of the laundry baskets they were using to pack books in the library. When she was settled, they ran up the stairs as fast as they could and, once inside the chapel, rushed to the door. To their horror they discovered it was locked. No doubt Natasha had the key. Theo and Nicholas looked stunned.

'God help us,' breathed Nicholas, 'it must still be with that witch.'

They descended the spiral staircase again at breakneck speed. When they entered the crypt, Theo shouted, 'Don't move, Maggie – we've had to come back for the chapel key.'

Feverishly they rushed to the coffin. As they got near, they were horrified by the sound of fists pounding the lid of the coffin from within. They unscrewed the lid of the coffin, and as they lifted it, Natasha started screaming at them and clawed the air with her manacled hands; her knuckles were raw and bleeding, her head resting in a pool of blood. Nicholas felt sick.

'Oh God, we can't leave her like this.'

Theo glared at him. 'Look for the key, you limey soft-head – I'll fix this screaming.' He turned to the statue in the niche behind the altar and tore off its black veil to reveal a perfect representation in alabaster of the Grand Master's face. Theo admitted later that its penetrating gaze overwhelmed him, but he had picked up one of the iron candlesticks and smashed the face of the statue. While he was doing this, Nicholas found the chapel key, removing it from a pocket in Natasha's skirt. Again she tried to claw at him, but the manacles on her wrists were too short to allow her to make contact. Theo made a gag out of the veil and tied it tightly round her screaming mouth and silenced her. Then they screwed down the coffin lid for the second time. Facing Nicholas over the coffin, Theo said, 'Buddy, I know what you're feeling, but we heard them say the burial was not until later this evening. They'll be contacted well before then. Let's get the hell out of here.'

The key unlocked the chapel door and they ran to the library, where Kirsten was loading books into one of the laundry baskets with Charlotte helping her. Both girls were shocked at the dishevelled appearance of the two men; both of them had shirts spattered with blood. Nicholas put a finger to his lips and in a whisper tried to explain the appalling horrors they had overheard. Stunned and pale, the girls were told what the plan was; their part in it was firstly to keep watch in the corridor until they returned with Maggie. He told them they were going to smuggle Maggie out in one of the laundry baskets, covered with a layer of books. They

111

would then bring it out of the chapel, if the coast was clear, to the nearby lift in the corridor. Theo had previously discovered that this lift went to the basement, where there was a storeroom; this had bolted double doors leading to the car park. Once the girls were clear about their roles, the two men returned to the chapel, locking the doors from within, and went down to the crypt. The hideous drumming on the lid of the coffin was continuing, but spasmodically.

They shouted to Maggie as they entered and she stumbled out of her hiding place. Theo seized one of her hands and dragged her up the stairs and led her to the laundry basket waiting above. Nicholas gingerly opened the chapel door and the two girls, who had been pretending to gossip outside, confirmed that the way was clear. Good fortune was with them, and they managed to get the basket out of the chapel unseen, and into the lift. They unbolted the double doors leading out of the storeroom and Nicholas ran to his car and backed it into the entrance. They lifted Maggie into the boot. This done, they closed the storeroom doors and, taking their two cars, all sped to their hotel. When they arrived they sent the girls to collect clean shirts from their rooms. They agreed that the management must not suspect them of leaving illicitly and they elected Nicholas to speak to the manager in the reception area, to explain that there was a sudden two-day seminar arranged at the Templar Castle, but that they would be back after it. In the meanwhile they would be clearing their rooms, which could be let in their absence. The manager had been understanding, saying the Templars were paying anyway, but he did suffer from them often changing their bookings.

They packed in record time and Theo risked using his special-issue mobile phone to ring Colonel Baker. He explained their horrific discoveries and also how they feared for their own safety. Colonel Baker occasionally gave a grunt of surprise as the tale unfolded but, rapidly grasping the situation, gave them his orders to enable them to escape. He would send an RAF plane to an airport near the Swiss–German border at Blumberg. The airport was some thirty miles over the border and the plane should be there in two and a half hours. Theo explained that their replacement of Maggie in the coffin meant that Lady Natasha's life would be extinguished instead of the girl's at eight o'clock that evening. In order that they should not be murderers, he asked Colonel Baker to contact the Templars and effect the release of the new occupant of the coffin. Theo also explained that they would be bringing Kirsten and Maggie.

Colonel Baker said, 'Excellent. I'll ring the Templars when I hear you are actually on the plane and the fact that you are bringing the Templar girl will provide us with vital inside information. Well done! We shall all meet at my office later tonight. I'll arrange cars to bring you straight from RAF Ruislip. It appears you've been successful, even at the last minute.'

After this call Theo had snorted, 'Bastard! Last minute indeed.'

They left the hotel at top speed, Kirsten travelling with Theo and Nicholas taking Charlotte and Maggie. They knew they were fleeing in fear of their lives, but added to their rapid exit was the knowledge that they possessed damning evidence against the evil of the Templar Order. All of them were slowly coming out of a state of shock which manifested itself in the trembling of Nicholas's hands and in Charlotte twisting a damp handkerchief, while Maggie groaned in the back of the car.

Charlotte turned to Maggie. 'I'm finding it very difficult to grasp what we've just learnt but can you explain the existence of the empty coffin in the crypt? It's the stuff of nightmares.'

Maggie answered in a low voice, almost hinting at a note of regret at a lost way of life, of belonging to a family. 'For two years those wishing to become full members of our Templar

Order have to serve as postulants. Until the last six months of that period, we act in the running of the Order with knowledge that it is a powerful charitable force: fund-raising for its new college near Zurzach and the hospital to be built in Jerusalem. However, in the last six months, if the novice master thinks fit, you will be groomed for full membership. Ah yes, these Templars are full of cunning. Subtly one is seduced by a Templar member and in the glow of romance and lust, led into the esoteric secrets of the Order. At that stage there is no going back, no leaving. In our secret temple in the crypt, an empty coffin is always on the altar of one of the chapels, a constant warning of the Order's ultimate sanction, burial alive, a disciplinary threat few dare to test.'

'Mother of God!' exclaimed Charlotte. 'How many have suffered this while you have been a Templar?'

Maggie answered, 'In my time, three, plus one reprieved. At the last minute the Grand Master can grant a reprieve just after the coffin has been lowered into the grave in the castle courtyard. The sentence is then changed to a period of solitary confinement in the castle dungeons. Anyway, I mentioned one reprieved, but when they opened the coffin, they found he had died of a heart attack.'

Nicholas muttered, 'It's beyond belief.'

Charlotte carried on her questioning. 'Why you, Maggie? How did you get condemned?'

'The Grand Master fancied me. I was one of many, but Lady Natasha caught me in his office while he was undoing my shirt, that's the real reason. After that the Indian Templars did the dirty work – you know they are "Thuggee" – before I knew it I had one of their ropes with a slip knot round my neck and woke up in the crypt.'

Nicholas butted in. 'You probably realise Theo and I got into the church when you left it unlocked. We got into the crypt by the time you were brought down. I'm afraid we heard worse than you being so cruelly treated. It's beyond belief! I don't know how much you know, but their plans are horrific, sheer evil, and it seems that under their Crusader veneer, they seek darker powers.'

Maggie leant forward in her seat at the back of the car. 'Ah yes: Lord Bahomet, we must be very careful, much prayer is needed to guard our souls. We are all in great danger.'

She spoke no longer as a terrified young woman; her voice was now calm and deliberate.

When she finished, Nicholas and Charlotte admitted later that a spiritual fear gripped them. Charlotte felt a pain at the pit of her stomach and panic rising like a mist through her body. Shortly after Charlotte's questioning of Maggie, they found themselves approaching the road to the Swiss/German border outside the Rhine town of Koblenz. The last two hundred yards to the border were an agony, especially for Nicholas and his passengers, as Maggie had revealed her lack of a passport. Theo, in the car in front of them, merely slowed as he approached the police checkpoint and held his passport out of the window, but had to stop suddenly as there was a flurry of activity around the car immediately in front of him. It's driver was dragged from his car and pulled into the border building by two policemen. Another policeman got into the empty car and drove it away. It was an unnerving moment for Theo, but another policeman came forward and waved him on. When Nicholas drew alongside, their hearts were thumping with fear, but the border policeman merely glanced at Maggie and, seeing her Templar uniform, saluted her. He then took Nicholas's passport to check it. Nicholas tried to control his trembling hand. The policeman nodded and said, 'OK – good journey. Sorry for the delay; we've been looking all day for the criminal in front – an escaped bankrupt.'

As they crossed the bridge they burst out laughing. Maggie said, 'Bankruptcy is worse than murder in Switzerland.'

14

After crossing the bridge they drove for half an hour until they found a café. They drove into its car park and, jumping out of their cars, ran towards each other and embraced. Tears of relief and joy mixed with their cries of happiness at having escaped. An hour and a half later, they parked their Templar cars at the airport, leaving them for their owners to collect. Like holidaymakers they entered the airport as if they had no cares in the world. They found an official who guided them to a room for passengers flying by private plane and there they were able to relax. When they explained it was an RAF plane, it was not necessary for them to complete any formalities and the lack of Maggie's passport was not an issue.

At the same time, it had just been noted in the Castle that their metal exit tabs had not been put in their slots at five o'clock. The Templar on security duty rang Count Alexei to report their omission. In the panic of their departure, they had given no thought to this problem. Count Alexei was drinking his third large Bloody Mary when he took the call. With a curse, he rang their hotel and, speaking to the manager, asked him to inform his guests that one of them must drive back to the Castle, *multi vivace*, to return their security tags. The manager expressed surprise and explained how they had recently checked out and that they had told him they were returning to the Castle for a two-day seminar.

Count Alexei sobered up immediately; there was something seriously amiss, but he gave nothing away. 'Of course, stupid of me to forget the seminar.' When he put his phone down, he pressed an alarm button on his desk. A few minutes later the Templar head of security burst in. Count

Alexei explained that the team had left with their tags. The explanation might be that they were having a rave-up in Zurich or Basle, but he needed to know where they were. He told the head of security to activate their car tracker system immediately, and let him know where they had got to.

Five minutes later Count Alexei's phone rang with the news that their two cars were stationary at Blumberg Airport car park. Count Alexei thanked him for this information. His mouth went dry with fear; something was very wrong. He took out a black address book from his desk, marked High Security Rating. He opened it at Blumberg Airport, but they did not have a permanent Templar operative in that small airport, though large nearby airports like Zurich, Basle or Munich were manned twenty-four hours a day by security members of the Order. He had therefore to alert the Templar nearest to Blumberg Airport. He was glad to see in his address book that a Herman von Schwab lived nearby: the book noted that he was a retired, high-ranking German police officer. Alexei's phone call to his house was not answered. Count Alexei began to panic. He had been made responsible for the researchers, and for the first two weeks of their stay, had kept them under observation by two trainee Templar security squad members. However the researchers working assiduously during the day, and leading a boring and blameless social life after hours, had led Count Alexei to suspend their surveillance. Now they had disappeared without warning and their Templar cars were parked at Blumberg Airport. If this was seriously bad news, he would be held responsible by the Grand Master; he would be reprimanded, even flogged or worse. Count Alexei looked at the address book again and saw that von Schwab had a mobile phone number, which he rang immediately.

Herman, the retired police officer, was reading a pin-up magazine away from his wife. By his side his mobile phone rang. Count Alexei wasted no time in telling him that getting hold of the researchers was a matter of the highest security threat to the Order. He added that as a highly respected member of the Order he expected Herman to attend to the matter immediately. He hoped that they had only just arrived at the airport, probably en route to London, via a larger German hub. Count Alexei gave their names and the reason why they must be instantly arrested and brought to the Castle at Zurzach; they had committed a serious criminal fraud against the Templars and they might spread slander against the Order to defend themselves. It was Herman von Schwab's task to apprehend them by whatever means necessary. If he failed, there would be serious consequences for him. Count Alexei repeated this threat.

Fortunately von Schwab knew the head policeman at the airport and managed to speak to him on his mobile phone. This policeman was at that moment patrolling the departure area of the airport. Knowing his retired colleague was a man of consequence led him to promise the greatest diligence in carrying out this task. With narrowed eyes he looked at the departure board; a charter flight was due to leave directly to London. It was in fact filling with contented tourists, who had just enjoyed a short break in the Black Forest. The aircraft was being boarded at that very moment. The policeman immediately issued orders to delay its departure and called up reinforcements to join him at the boarding gate. Once there, his gimlet eyes scanned the passenger list and saw there was a Miss Fox travelling on that flight. He had only been given the fugitives' surnames, and assumed the others would be travelling under false names.

'Got one of them,' he said to one of his police team. 'Let's go.' As a precaution he drew his pistol and surged on to the plane to the dismay of the charter flight crew. There was no seating plan. Miss Fox was over eighty and deaf. She was at the back of the plane trying to do a crossword. So absorbed was she that she did not notice the arrival of the police, nor due to her deafness did she hear the stewardess call her name, asking her to put up a hand. As there was no reaction the policeman barked all their names, ordering them to stand up at once. Again there was no reaction. To the policeman, this proved their guilt. The captain of the aircraft appeared and accompanied the policeman to check each passenger's identity. Eventually, at the back of the plane, they found the unconcerned Miss Fox, who, asked to prove her identity by the captain, was surprised when, having done so, she was frogmarched off the plane by a policeman with a pistol.

While these precious minutes had been wasted in this wild goose chase, the party destined for London courtesy of the RAF were in the air enjoying champagne, ordered by Colonel Baker.

Nicholas rang the Colonel to tell him of their safe departure at seven o'clock. Captain Patricia took the message, as the Colonel was elsewhere reporting developments to Brigadier Jackson.

At the same time the coffin was being moved by four of the Indians from the crypt to the chapel above. They rested there waiting, before moving it to the courtyard. They assumed Lady Natasha would be awaiting its arrival there. They expected later to be richly rewarded by her. Muffled groans came from within the coffin, which had been dragged up the spiral staircase. At a quarter to eight the coffin began its slow journey to the castle courtyard. The bearers could hear the steady beat of the drums as they got nearer; hearing this sound, the occupant of the coffin began piteously crying and beating again on the lid.

At seven-forty-five, Colonel Baker entered his office. Captain Patricia put her head round the door.

'Good news, our heroes have just left Blumberg Airport. I suppose with the drive from RAF Ruislip they should arrive here just before midnight.'

Colonel Baker's face broke into a smile. 'This is going to

be the start of a real bust.' He glanced at his watch. 'My God! I nearly forgot – I've only got a few minutes to save a life. Try and get the Templar Castle on the phone at once. Before doing this, can you get the Russian Count's mobile number, the Templar cove in charge of our team there?'

Captain Patricia disappeared into her nearby office and quickly reappeared with the mobile number. It was seven-fifty.

Colonel Baker said, 'You ring the main Templar number while I ring the Count.'

As he did so the Count was making his way from his beloved library office towards the courtyard. Before leaving he had drunk a fourth large vodka. The Count had a dread of these burials, being claustrophobic himself. These events gave him nightmares for days after.

The Templars were beginning to chant the name Bahomet. The coffin was now resting on struts by the open grave in the centre of the courtyard. Luckily for Lady Natasha, the Count, in his intoxicated condition, had brought his mobile phone with him under the black Templar robe in which all those in the courtyard were likewise dressed. Just before he entered the courtyard, he stopped to steady himself; he planned to stand as far away as possible. It was then that his phone rang. Hurriedly he went back into the corridor – mobile phones being absolutely forbidden. He answered it, hoping it was news from Blumberg Airport. He went ashen as he heard the speaker.

'My name is irrelevant but I am head of a department in the British Intelligence Services investigating your Order. When I finish my call you can ring back and our exchange will confirm that this is the War Office. I have information that three researchers, an American librarian and a Templar, Sergeant Maggie, have recently left Blumberg Airport. They will report here later.'

Count Alexei gasped, 'Sergeant Maggie!'

Colonel Baker continued, 'Immediately though, I have to tell you that one of your manic Grand Master's mistresses called Natasha is in a coffin and about to be buried alive instead of Sergeant Maggie. Good-night.'

Count Alexei's hand trembled so much that he had dropped the phone. He sank to the floor of the corridor, slumped against the wall. He considered letting the burial of Natasha continue – no one would know it was not Maggie. The drums in the courtyard were quickening and the chant of 'Bahomet' rose in volume. Count Alexei had to abandon his idea as he remembered he had given Maggie's name to their man von Schwab. His nightmare reverie was interrupted by the Templar treasurer hurrying down the corridor. He stopped in front of Count Alexei, still slumped on the floor.

'The GM sent me to fetch Lady Natasha; as it's her show he's angry at her absence. Have you seen her?'

The Count raised his head and in a slurred voice he said, 'She's not absent. She's in the coffin.'

The treasurer's jaw dropped; colour drained from his face. 'What? Repeat that if you dare. What the hell are you doing slumped on the ground? Alexei, you're a drunken sot! Get up. We must stop the burial at once.' He dragged the Count to his feet and into the courtyard with the Count mumbling, 'Terrible mistake, sorry, sorry.'

The drums gave a long rolling sound, ending in a climactic final beat, like a gunshot. The chanting stopped. The Grand Master stepped forward and nodded to the four Indians who had brought in the coffin to bring it to the edge of the grave; they slid strong red silk ropes under it and lifted it off its stand to the edge. The only sound was that of doves on the castle roof as they flirted with each other. Suddenly the crowd could hear the last desperate thumping from within the coffin.

The treasurer's attempt to get the Count to accompany him

failed; he had been dragging Alexei forward by the sleeve of his robe, and it was torn off as the Russian resisted. All eyes in the courtyard, except those of the Grand Master, turned towards the struggling men as the sound of the tearing robe intruded on their state of near religious ecstasy.

The Grand Master was intoning a series of curses and had just raised his right arm; the coffin was lifted over the grave, supported by the Indians on either side holding the red ropes. They had been instructed that when the Grand Master lowered his arm, they were to let the coffin sink gracefully into the grave.

They were distracted as the treasurer let out a terrific cry. 'Stop! Stop at once! Lady Natasha is in the coffin. Stop, please … '

The Grand Master's dignified ceremonial role was shattered in that moment. From an expression of calm command it changed to one of horror. His raised right arm fell to his side. The Indians hesitated for a moment but felt that obedience to the ritual was sacrosanct; the coffin descended below with a rush. The treasurer reached the side of the Grand Master and conveyed the news that Alexei had just given him. For a brief moment they whispered to each other and the treasurer moved to the middle of the courtyard.

'Everyone to their quarters. The ceremony is postponed and also the party afterwards. The Grand Master requests the Council go to his office in half an hour.' The treasurer went over to the Indians. 'Get the coffin up immediately and take it to the Grand Master's dressing room. Be careful but quick.' He then gave orders to two of the Templar security team, who went over to Count Alexei, still slumped in the corridor. They handcuffed his wrists behind his back and marched him to the Grand Master's office. The deputy master, Karl, followed behind and went into the dressing room adjoining the Grand Master's office as the coffin appeared.

Two Templar nurses joined them to assist in the recovery of Lady Natasha. Between them they were carrying a stretcher, and as she was removed from the coffin they placed her on it. She was bruised, soiled and hysterical. Karl wanted to go to her and show his love.

In sharp contrast, the Grand Master did not speak a word, his expression impassive.

After Lady Natasha had been taken to the infirmary, he said to Karl, 'Come and sit my side of the table while we hear what Count Alexei has to say for himself.'

Still handcuffed, the Russian was brought in. His fear had made him sober so that he was able to repeat the message he had received from Colonel Baker word for word. He gave no satisfactory explanation as to how the switch in the coffin could have taken place, though he had to say that he had seen Karl and Natasha entering the chapel together that afternoon. The expression on the Grand Master's face hardened.

'Count Alexei, you have failed appallingly. I believe somewhere in this terrible failure we shall find that our researchers are somehow involved. Until the picture is clearer you will be confined below in the solitary wing of the dungeons.' He pressed a button on his table and the security men took him away, protesting loudly.

The Grand Master turned to Karl. 'Explain! How do I know it wasn't you who put Natasha in the coffin, caused by a lovers' tiff, perhaps. Don't think I didn't notice your concern for her a moment ago.'

Karl laughed nervously. 'Don't be absurd. Natasha wanted company while she checked the coffin; naturally she would have preferred you to have been there, but you were away. When we were satisfied that all was in order, we went to the bar; others were there, including the treasurer. We had a drink with him and then Natasha went to her room while I had a meeting with our Teutonic brothers.'

The Grand Master leant back in his chair. 'Of course I'll check your story, and if it's true, then I'm very glad. We have a crisis and we have to trust each other within the Council. We have to move on to a war footing. Get the British Grand Master informed and tell him to be ruthless, even reckless, in eliminating the two Americans, the two English and of course, above all, Sergeant Maggie. It's also essential to find out who it is in British intelligence that rang Alexei; in fact he must be eliminated first. I have someone high up in British intelligence and, if I remember rightly, during some of his career he ran a successful campaign assassinating IRA members. Our Jerusalem project must proceed, of course, only known to the Council. It is imperative that no one else is to have knowledge of our plans.'

Karl went cold: he had discussed them with Natasha in the crypt. He convinced himself that they could not have been overheard, as Sergeant Margaret, in the coffin, was too far away from them. He would have to warn Natasha that they had been under suspicion and that she should make no mention of the Jerusalem project.

15

When the travellers from Germany arrived in Colonel Baker's office, they were welcomed with great bonhomie. Champagne corks popped and Captain Patricia had been instructed to get first-class snacks from an outside caterer. They were told that they would all be staying the night in War Office guest rooms so that they could start early the next day for a full debriefing. They were taken to these rooms to freshen up before they settled down to make a brief report over the refreshments. This gathering would take place in Brigadier Jackson's office. To Colonel Baker's annoyance, the Brigadier had decided to muscle in on the debriefing. The Colonel suspected that the Brigadier was after some of the glory as well as the champagne.

Although the travellers were drained by the events of the day they were still buoyed up by the realisation that they had escaped from the Templars. This sense of relief was dampened when Colonel Baker told them that the first priority would be their own protection: secure housing would be a necessity for several days and probably weeks.

Much to the Colonel's further annoyance, Brigadier Jackson interrupted this line of discussion. He said that the next day he had to be judging at an important horse trial and therefore had some questions to which he needed an immediate answer. He was particularly anxious to know the date and exact plan for the Jerusalem attack. Neither Nicholas nor Theo could supply this information, save that an Israeli helicopter would be landing to pick up the bomb. Theo had heard that much, but only a fragment of the name of the landing place; he would rack his brains to try and remember the Arabic place name, and unfortunately neither of them had heard the date.

The Brigadier raised his eyebrows. 'Well, that's a bit of a bugger.'

Later Charlotte was to recall that he did not seem to be really put out by this lack of critical information. His next questions concentrated on what they had discovered about the Templars, particularly their custom of using the threat of burial alive to control their members.

The Brigadier's interrogation was cut short by the appearance of the War Office doctor who had given them information on brainwashing. He immediately ordered Sergeant Maggie to bed and gave her some pills to ease her pain and help her sleep. He told Charlotte he would see her next day so that she could debrief him on her experience and he could help her recover her memory.

Colonel Baker then congratulated them all and confirmed they would meet again next morning, but he handed them a questionnaire to complete beforehand. He wanted to correlate their experiences so that he could present a cohesive picture of the Templar operation.

When they gathered together in his office the next day, Captain Patricia took Sergeant Maggie to her own office so that she could extract more details of the Templars: how they recruited new members and how they led them into the cultish aspect of the Order and its depraved rituals. Most importantly, the criminal evidence relating to their burial-alive activities needed a full statement so that the Swiss authorities could act immediately. Patricia asked Maggie how many burials had taken place during her five years as a full member of the Templar Order. Maggie said there had been three, one of which was of the Arab assassin who had attempted to kill the Grand Master in the Dolder Grande Hotel.

It became apparent to Patricia that the Grand Master still

had a strong emotional hold over Maggie; every time she mentioned him, she showed great psychological stress. Patricia concluded that Maggie was rationalising her horrific experience as being organised by the jealousy of the mistress of the Grand Master, Lady Natasha. Patricia feared that she was emotionally fixated; the Templars had become her family and the Grand Master her beloved leader. Patricia concluded they would have to keep a close watch on her in case she convinced herself that she would be in no danger if she returned to the Templar Castle. As Patricia's fears increased, she told Maggie they would have a break. Patricia immediately joined Colonel Baker and the others, who were discussing the contents of their questionnaire. She took Colonel Baker aside and he quickly agreed that Maggie could prove unreliable and unstable. Colonel Baker said the solution was simple: they would insist that she go into hiding in a safe house for her own security, but in effect, it would be a prison for Maggie until the Templar Order was eliminated.

Colonel Baker brought the discussions with the others to a rapid close. He had arranged for a plane to take him from RAF Ruislip to Zurich to meet with the Swiss Security Services. He would leave when signed statements from the four escapees and Maggie had been signed; these he would take with him in the hope that criminal action would start immediately against the Templars.

Colonel Baker made Patricia responsible for the safety of Nicholas and Charlotte. The previous night he had had a conference call with the CIA in America as Theo and Kirsten wished to return to the USA: therefore they had become the responsibility of the American state.

Patricia began by telling them they could not return to Cambridge for some weeks; their colleges would be informed, but they would have to be secure in a safe house, which would be a restrictive experience and they might have to be moved frequently, like Salman Rushdie, and maybe have their appearances altered. As witnesses to the criminality of the Templars, every effort would be made to eliminate the two of them.

Charlotte interrupted to ask if she and Nicholas could have a private discussion, as she had a suggestion to make. Patricia took them to the empty office of Brigadier Jackson, who was attending his horse trial, which seemed to have taken precedence over alerting the Israeli authorities to the threat to the Dome of the Mosque in Jerusalem.

Charlotte told Nicholas that her sister Sarah had married into a rich Yorkshire family who, in addition to owning three thousand acres of the North York moors, had a manor house in a secluded valley there. This manor house had a nearby cottage away from public view. They would be safe there and her sister's in-laws were a jovial family so that there would be some social life. Charlotte was certain they could be trusted. It was a free country and unless Colonel Baker arrested them, they surely had a choice as to where they might hide safely. Nicholas agreed wholeheartedly. They returned to Patricia and got her agreement in principle, though she said she would have to consult with Colonel Baker, who was about to leave for his flight to Zurich. Colonel Baker joined them and asked Patricia to find an Ordnance Survey map to show the location of the manor house. In a few minutes, Patricia produced the Ordnance Survey Explorer map, OL26, on which Charlotte pinpointed the house's position, close to the hamlet of Hawnby. Colonel Baker smiled benignly.

'I've been grouse shooting there, country wild as a hawk. You should be OK. Change your names, your hairstyle and wear dark glasses if you have to go out. Whatever you do you must not tell anyone, family or friends, where you are. Perhaps, Charlotte, you could use the Brigadier's office again to contact your sister and clear the way to your going there. While you are doing that, Patricia and I will contact your colleges and tell them to send any correspondence or messages via Patricia.' Nicholas went with Charlotte to see whether she would be successful in their request.

Her sister thought there would be no problem, but was naturally alarmed to think that there was some threat. While they were awaiting confirmation that they would be welcome at her in-laws' cottage, Colonel Baker burst in; his face was flushed and his steely calm was absent as he sat down. He was breathing heavily.

'I've just rung your Master of Michaelhouse, Canon Frobisher, to tell him you will be out of direct contact for some weeks. I'm afraid there has been a serious development – the Templars are moving fast. Your Master was in a frightful state. Someone primed your music centre with an electrical device that delivered a killing shock through the 'on/off' switch. Evidently some bogus character came to the college on the pretence that you had instructed him to mend your music centre. I'm afraid someone else took the killing shock ... '

Nicholas was so stunned that he couldn't find the words to question this extraordinary announcement. Charlotte was ashen, but putting her hand on Nicholas's arm, managed to speak. 'How was this discovered?'

Colonel Baker sighed. 'A fellow member of your college took the rap – one Frederick Clegg; has a room on your staircase, I understood. Your bedder found him dead, lying by your music centre, dead from a massive electric shock, his hand by the "on/off" switch; arm burned and clothes scorched. It must have been a massive charge.'

Nicholas and Charlotte looked at each other, aghast. Nicholas felt guilty as he suspected Clegg might have been trying to sabotage his hated playing of Gilbert and Sullivan. He wondered whether Clegg had been the cause of his own horrible death. Nicholas uttered this thought.

Colonel Baker shook his head. 'I think not. Your Canon

Frobisher called the police and their initial report was that it was a very sophisticated device, boosting the electrical charge – and of course there's the mystery of the visiting electrician. I think now you will appreciate the need for a safe haven. Best of luck – I have to rush to Ruislip now. Patricia is your link while I am away.' He shook their hands and was gone.

Nicholas leant forward, burying his face in his hands.

'No doubt Clegg was up to no good in my rooms, but he didn't deserve that.'

Charlotte, standing behind him, put her arms round his waist and nuzzled the back of his neck; her face was wet with tears. They did not speak; they were both in a state of shock, thinking about what might have happened. Their reverie was broken by the arrival of Patricia bearing a welcome cup of tea. Colonel Baker had told her the news before he left, and she fussed over them in a solicitous manner. She told them they were to stay another night and that next morning a car would be available so that they could drive to North York-shire. They were forbidden to use their credit cards or cheque books and if they would come to her office before leaving, they would be given two thousand pounds each in cash to cover the cost of renewing their wardrobes and their living expenses. She had arranged that their colleges would forward all correspondence to her and she would deal with their bills as they came in.

She had checked that their special-issue mobile phones would work around the area of Helmsley, as they would be living nearby. As they parted she said with a sly laugh that they would have ample time for undisturbed study.

The Master of the English Templars had other plans for them, providing he could discover their whereabouts.

16

Sir Darcy de Malplaquet gave his secretary the task of finding Nicholas and Charlotte. She had no success enquiring about Nicholas at Michaelhouse, nor would they reveal the address of his next of kin.

However, she had better luck in locating Charlotte. She had rung Newnham College, but unfortunately the instructions not to reveal any details had not yet reached the Porter's Office and they told her that Charlotte had a vacation address near Sevenoaks and that her next of kin was a sister at that address, Sarah Adamson.

In point of fact, Sarah had married well and lived in a fine house in the Surrey countryside. This house had a cottage in the grounds for which Charlotte paid a peppercorn rent. Her brother-in-law worked in the City and Charlotte nicknamed him 'Soames', as he was a typical Galsworthy character.

The Templar secretary found, on ringing directory enquiries, that the number was ex-directory. However the Templars had an insider in BT who took ten minutes to come back to her with the number. She rang it. A child answered.

'Mummy is out, she's gone to the garden centre – it's the third time this week.'

The secretary put on her most coaxing manner. 'Is your Mummy called Charlotte?'

'No that's my Auntie, she's lovely, and she's just sent me some chocs from Switzerland. They were in a beautiful box with a picture of lovely mountains.' The child was bored, having been left alone, and welcomed a chat.

The secretary persisted. 'Is she still in Switzerland? I have some important news for her. Do you know where she is?'

There was a long pause. 'Are you a friend?'

'Yes, a very good friend.'

There was a further silence until the small voice answered in a confidential tone, 'Well – Auntie had a long talk with Mummy yesterday and afterwards Mummy said she would not be coming to her cottage here but going to my Granddaddy in Yorkshire. He is lovely too, Granddaddy Rupert.'

The secretary seized her chance. 'Wonderful, we can get our important news to her there. What's your Granddaddy's name and where does he live?'

A further period of quiet. She heard the child saying, 'Eeny Meeny Miny Mo ... '

The secretary interrupted. 'What's your name, by the way?'

A further pause. 'Samantha, but they call me Sam.'

'Sam, it's very important to know where she is. I'm trying to help your Auntie.'

The answer came slowly, as if the child was reciting a solemn speech in a school play.

'Granddaddy is called Rupert Fortesque and he lives at Fortesque Hall near lots of big moors. Auntie C says I'm cool. Goodbye.'

The secretary quickly recorded this minimal information and immediately tried directory enquiries to locate a Rupert Fortesque in various North Country areas. She was lucky: Rupert Fortesque lived in Fortesque Hall, near Helmsley, a North Yorkshire moors market town. She immediately rang Darcy de Malplaquet and gave him this information. He in turn lost no time in ringing the Grand Master of the Teutonic Knights in Berlin. He knew they had a specially trained hit squad for the task he had in mind. He obtained immediate co-operation from Berlin: their squad would fly to Teeside Airport, ostensibly to cull deer on behalf of the Forestry Commission. Malplaquet wasted no time, arranged transport to meet the party at the airport and himself set out from Temple Guiting to meet them there later that day.

While these arrangements were being made, Nicholas and

Charlotte were making their way to Captain Patricia's office to collect their money and any last-minute instructions. They knocked on her door, but hearing no reply, walked in. They found her slumped over her desk, her head resting on her arms and sobbing convulsively. She raised her head, waved them to sit down, and muttering, 'Sorry,' disappeared into Colonel Baker's adjoining office. Nicholas and Charlotte looked at each other in amazement, but before they could speak, Patricia put her head round the door and said, 'It's Richard: they got him last night on the way to the airport, bomb in the boot, blew the car in half. Oh God, God ... ' She disappeared back into Colonel Baker's office.

Nicholas and Charlotte sat in stunned silence.

'Crikey, they don't waste time – Clegg first, now Colonel Baker. I'm beginning to welcome our disappearance, the quicker the better,' said Nicholas.

Further discussion was made impossible by the appearance of the doctor, followed by Patricia. He explained that they would help her through this horrific period, but an orderly would appear to take them to their car shortly. Patricia had stopped crying but with red, swollen eyes, looked dishevelled; even so, she had herself under control and went to a safe in the corner of the room, and removed two fat envelopes, which she gave to Nicholas and Charlotte. She told them to take extra care and even managed a smile as she instructed them not to blow the cash all at once. With her mouth set rigid, she added it would be her life's task to settle the score with the Templars. Brigadier Jackson would take over the direction of the campaign when he came back next day from judging horses. Until otherwise decided, she would be their first point of contact, and she would check with them every day.

An Army sergeant appeared and told them he would take them to their car. Patricia put her arms around their necks and, sobbing again, wished them, 'God speed!' They themselves were overcome and could only wave goodbye as they followed the sergeant to collect their car. Ten minutes later, they drove out of the back of the War Office and travelled along the Embankment until they reached Blackfriars Bridge; here they joined Farringdon Road to head north.

Four and a half hours later, they had driven from the A1 to Thirsk and from there made the dramatic climb up Sutton Bank to see the North York moors shimmering in late-afternoon sun. From there they felt they were almost gliding as they travelled down the long road to Helmsley. In the middle of this pleasant town, there was an open market area, and overlooking this, the Black Swan Hotel. Here they parked and went inside to enjoy a hotel tea. They sat in an area near to the hotel reception and overheard the raised voices of some of the staff, who were complaining about a last-minute booking for fourteen rooms for a German shooting party. One of them said, 'It's not bloody grouse-shooting time yet, not until August … ' This exchange was of no significance to Nicholas and Charlotte, save that their tea took a long time to come.

After tea, feeling refreshed, they spent some of their money kitting themselves out in the manner of tourists to the area, though both gave themselves the bonus of tweed jackets in case they were under-dressed on occasion in their new country setting. Nicholas had also found a shop where he could buy a large-scale map of the area. After loading their shopping bags into the car, Nicholas was able to pinpoint the exact location of Fortesque Hall: it lay in what appeared to be an empty valley, beyond the small hamlet of Hawnby, a few miles off the Helmsley–Rydale road. Out of Helmsley they climbed again on to the moors and on passing a sign to Rievaulx Abbey noted it as a future day out. As they continued, the moors appeared to stretch away to infinity, shimmering in a purple haze. For a moment the enchantment banished their horrific memories: Nicholas slowed the car and drove off the road on to a track. This crossed the moor to a small coppice of wind-bent pines. Reaching the trees, they stopped to stretch their legs. Nearby a grouse gave a staccato grumbling call and in the distance a curlew added its plaintive song. They walked round the wood and on the other side Nicholas took Charlotte's hand and drew her to him.

'I understand from what you've told me that our host bubbles with rumbustious enjoyment of life, but your sister's mother-in-law is an austere follower of the Italian Mission of which you are a member. I suspect she may thwart my desire to share our hidden cottage together after dark – so ... ' They moved together and kissed passionately, to a background of further grumbling calls from the nearby grouse. Ten minutes later they brushed heather from their clothes and walked back round the wood to the car. As the main road came into view again, Charlotte seized Nicholas by the hand and pulled him behind the nearest trees. She had seen a convoy of three black limousines coming from the north, down the main road to Helmsley, each one filled with dark-suited men sitting upright in regimented rows behind the drivers. The sun was behind them as it was beginning its evening descent to the western horizon: it illuminated the interiors of the cars and the sight disturbed them. It was unpleasantly reminiscent of the large cars the Templars used in Switzerland. Charlotte instinctively whispered, 'I think we should get to our Shangri-La as soon as possible – those cars gave me the creeps.'

Nicholas felt a twinge of panic but tried to lighten the moment. 'Probably they were just reinforcements going to your Ampleforth Abbey.' He tried to kiss her again.

'Fruitcake,' was her practical response. 'Let's go.'

The cars they had seen contained the Teutonic Knights from Berlin and Darcy de Malplaquet and his assistant, Fred. Malplaquet had also taken the precaution of warning customs at Teeside Airport that this shooting party would be bringing their own guns. In spite of this, when inspecting their luggage, eyebrows were raised at the high calibre of their rifles and their attached telescopic sights. Their story seemed in order when customs were told they were staying in the Black Swan in Helmsley, a hotel well known for accommodating shooting parties. Malplaquet had made arrangements for them all to dine in a private room in the hotel. Unfortunately it was not far enough away from the mainly aged guests to muffle the sound of raucous German drinking songs. Complaints were made to the manager on duty, but the strongly built appearance of the Germans drained his courage in reprimanding their behaviour.

At Fortesque Hall a riotous evening had also been enjoyed, but of higher quality. On arrival, Nicholas and Charlotte had been warmly welcomed, but Mrs Fortesque had made it plain that Charlotte would be their house guest while Nicholas would occupy the cottage. As they received this news, they heard the sound approaching of a fine tenor, singing, 'I am a captain of the Queen's navy … ' and they were joined by the roly-poly figure of their host. His head was topped by a mop of untidy white hair and his rubicund face creased in a smile of welcome. 'Hello! Hello and welcome. I'm Rupert and a special hello and kiss to Charlotte.' He wrapped his arms around her and gave her a hug, then turning to Nicholas, grasped his proffered right hand, covering it with his own two large hands. 'I'm looking forward to some lively discussion with you young things, even though you don't hail from Oxford.' He laughed loudly, before turning around at the sound of a discreet cough. 'Well now, here's our treasure, Mrs Pontefract – I call her "Liquorice". She'll take Charlotte and her luggage and in a minute, Philip, her husband, will take you, Nicholas, to the cottage. We'll all meet in half an hour in the sitting room and joust the night away on a sea of champers!' Rupert rubbed his hands in pleasurable anticipation. 'After dinner, snooker, and an evening of political and religious dispute, no doubt – see you later.' He waved at them and disappeared down the corridor, following his wife and singing, 'Where be ye going, dear little maiden? With your red rosy cheeks and black shiny hair ... ' then singing in falsetto, 'I'm going a milking, dear little man, she said, it's dabbling in the dew makes the milkmaids fair ... '

Charlotte went off with Mrs Pontefract to her room and her husband, Philip, appeared and picked up Nicholas's luggage after shaking his hand with a dinner-plate-sized fist, saying, 'Master is in good heart tonight, sir; he likes company, especially young'ns. He gets lonely just with his Missus, though in addition to you, young Mr Sebastian will soon be here from Oxford. Hey up, let's get thee to tha cottage.'

They went round the back of the house. Nicholas could see a line of stables ending in a large barn; there was no cottage to be seen. However, beyond the barn the ground sloped away down to a simple stone cottage, backed by an oak wood. Inside it was painted white; it contained a kitchen with oak cupboards and a large sitting room made up the rest of the ground floor. In this sitting room there was a wood-burning stove and chintz armchairs. Upstairs were two bedrooms and a bathroom. The stove had been lit downstairs so the cottage was warm and welcoming. Upstairs it smelt of scented soap. Philip had gone ahead turning on the lights and also pointing to two large torches in the kitchen; he explained there was no external lighting between the cottage and the main house. He left Nicholas to bathe and change and gather strength for the evening ahead.

Later when Nicholas arrived in the sitting room of the house, he found Charlotte already there, talking to Sebastian. Rupert and his wife were plumping up cushions on the numerous chairs and sofas. Rupert introduced the young man to Nicholas, saying, 'Another in-law for Charlotte; he's an afterthought and a pretty good one! He's coming down from Merton next year and thinking of joining his old school, Ampleforth, as a novice. His mother's ecstatic!' He smiled wryly and the young Sebastian blushed.

The room had a collection of portraits of former Fortesques, one a handsome Laurence portrait of a Cardinal Fortesque, plus small portraits of impossibly pious nuns – these competed with pictures of horses and square eighteenth-century cattle, so out of proportion that they looked like oil tankers compared to their surroundings. Over the fireplace was a medieval Florentine Madonna, labelled as by the Master of the Mineato. There was a gentle knock on the door and Mr and Mrs Pontefract entered. Rupert rapped his knuckles on a side table. 'Angelus time.' They all turned to face the Madonna.

'You lead us tonight, Sebastian,' purred his mother.

The Angelus prayer was said quickly and with such gusto that Nicholas felt no awkwardness in this throwback to family prayers which included anyone in the house. Mr and Mrs Pontefract slipped away to prepare dinner and Rupert placed himself foursquare in front of the fireplace, in which a fragrant log fire smouldered; he launched into a series of provocative remarks. His first was that loudspeakers should be placed on top of Catholic and Anglican churches and that the Angelus should be broadcast morning, noon and night so as to, 'sock it to the Mossis'. This caused some hilarity and Nicholas remarked that no doubt the populace at large would suffer stress and call on health and safety regulations, as was already happening in some areas where church bells were rung. Rupert was not deterred and changed the subject; his next suggestion was that everything should be done to encourage global warming, since it would be a positive advantage for the UK and he looked forward to a future in which Mediterranean fruits would flourish in North Yorkshire. He was fed up with the hype on the subject, considering the fact that there had been no significant increase in average temperature since the new century had begun. This started a more animated discussion than his Angelus suggestion, but it was brought to a close when their hostess told her husband that when he finished his third round of champagne, they should go into dinner.

Over dinner, Rupert told them that on the following day they had an annual invasion of Army cadets doing manoeuvres on the moors under the direction of the local regiment. He elaborated. 'Super day: the Army bring armoured cars, Jeeps and lots of thunder flashes and machine guns firing blanks. We all career about the moors and end the day with a party on the lawn if we're lucky with the weather. Nicholas and Charlotte, you will be very welcome to join me in one of the armoured cars.'

Sebastian laughed and said, 'Dad puts on a beret and thinks he's Montgomery!'

Dinner was consumed aided by a tide of claret and the noise of their discussions rose exponentially; even their hostess became quite giggly. After dinner, Rupert led them to the billiard room, where he declared that he and Sebastian would play Nicholas and Charlotte. Rupert's method of play was con brio, con whisky, con curses, con bellows of laughter. While they were not playing, Nicholas and Charlotte sat on a window seat holding hands like young lovers, briefly oblivious of the reasons as to why they had come to this eccentric refuge.

It was after midnight when the game ended. Rupert and his son said they would walk Nicholas back to his cottage, but first Rupert took him to his gun room which, in addition to reinforced metal gun cabinets, was cluttered with fishing rods and boots. Rupert produced a key ring and unlocked the cabinet, revealing a row of guns.

'Do yer shoot?' he asked Nicholas.

'Hardly,' replied Nicholas, 'the occasional pheasant, that sort of thing.'

Rupert looked a bit surprised, as if every self-respecting man should own two thousand acres of grouse moor. He picked out two guns, which he gave to Sebastian to hold.

'Charlotte gave us a brief outline of the danger you have escaped from, but you might sleep better with one of these by your side – one is a twelve-bore, the other a twenty-; the latter is easier to handle.' Rupert handed the gun to Nicholas with a bag of cartridges. When they got outside, the sky was absolutely clear and the surroundings lit by a full moon. 'Bloody marvellous God,' murmured Rupert. 'No light pollution here to spoil the show.'

When they reached the cottage they went in with Nicholas to check that the wooden shutters were secure inside the windows and advised him to bolt the doors behind them when they left. Soon afterwards, Nicholas was in bed, but unused to the quantity of drink consumed that evening, found that his head spun when he lay down. He could hear owls calling in the nearby woods and, taking a glass of water, went to his bedroom window, opening the shutters to admire the view. Although the cottage was surrounded on three sides by the woods, in front of it was a fine view up the hill, which at the top, led on to the moors. The moonlight made it look like a stage set. It was utterly still apart from the distant sound of the bleating of sheep.

This idyllic moment was disturbed by the sound of a car coming down the long hill from the main road. Curiously, though, Nicholas could see no lights from the car and its sound diminished to freewheeling with the engine switched off, before ceasing suddenly. Nicholas heard a click like a car door being shut gently; it was difficult to judge how far away it was.

During the riotous evening Nicholas had assumed that there could be no threat to themselves now that they were safely tucked away in an obscure cul-de-sac off the North York moors. He had had no intuition of any danger hearing the sound of the car; his only passing thoughts were that it could have been a car being driven by someone who had decided to sleep off too much alcohol, rather than risk going through Helmsley, or of lovers looking for the refuge of a moorland lay-by. He went back to bed and put out his light, leaving the window open. Usually he went to sleep quickly, but it eluded him that night. In this safe haven, offering comfort and friendly hosts, his mind had relaxed, but in his wakefulness his mind was invaded by a pent-up flood of horrific memories; his mind was particularly haunted by visions of Clegg, electrocuted by his music centre in his Cambridge rooms. Try as he might, he could not rid himself of some feelings of responsibility. He reasoned that a murder attempt intended for him but deflected to Clegg must have been the work of the bogus Malplaquet and his obscene Templar cult. Why should he be bearing this burden alone? The murderer should know they had killed an innocent man. Nicholas grew angrier; he was overwrought and, in this state of mind, decided to unload his rage. He remembered Malplaquet had given him his card and that it had had his mobile number on it, in addition to the address of the Temple Guiting Preceptory. Nicholas made a snap decision: he would leave a message on Malplaquet's mobile – a message that would give him an unpleasant shock. Nicholas put on his light, found his briefcase and Malplaquet's phone number. He punched this number into his mobile, put out his light and went to the open window. The owls were still calling to each other and he thought they would make a good background to his message. With a strong signal at the open window, he activated the number and leant forward to deliver his vitriolic message. He never sent it; simultaneously to hearing it connect, he also heard a mobile phone ringing between the cottage and the woods. It was immediately cut off and Nicholas heard a stifled expletive. Nicholas stumbled back from his open window and sat on his bed in a state of shock. It was impossible, he thought, that Malplaquet had discovered their hidden place of safety, not only discovered it, but had got there on the night of their arrival. He was outside at that very moment – how many others were with him? Nicholas was very, very frightened.

In the dark he went to the cupboard where he had placed the gun and then to the chest of drawers to collect the cartridges. He loaded the gun, and returned to the open window and peered out of one side; he saw two shadowy figures climbing away up the slope in front of the cottage, followed by the diminishing sound of running on the gravel drive beyond. Nicholas stood by the window, hardly able to breathe because of the terror of the moment, but a few minutes later, sighed with relief as he heard a car going away up to the main road. He stood at the window until he could hear the car no longer, then, clutching the gun, collapsed on the bed. He tried to decide whether they were leaving to get reinforcements to return that night or the next day, or if Malplaquet might have abandoned whatever plans he had. Nicholas was too tired to decide, but concluded that to report this visitation to the main house might only cause unnecessary panic; if they called the police, what proof did he have and would they believe his extraordinary story, that he and Charlotte were targets of assassins? He would have to consult Captain Patricia first. These questions whirled through his brain but were never answered – a merciful sleep intervened.

17

Nicholas was woken by Charlotte bringing him a cup of tea, but as the doors were locked, she had resorted to throwing gravel at his window. The noise woke him and the horror of the previous night possessed him. Grasping his gun, he peered out of the window to see Charlotte about to throw another handful of gravel. She burst out laughing as she saw him holding the gun. He went downstairs immediately and once she was inside, bolted the door. He told her to sit at the kitchen table and he cupped the tea with his hands as if to draw strength from it and then told her the alarming news of Malplaquet's visitation. As she grasped the news, fear also struck Charlotte; her voice trembled as she spoke.

'I am sorry the nightmare has come back so soon.'

He nodded. 'We'll have to tell Rupert. This is putting them all in danger as well.'

Charlotte was silent for a moment. 'Like Salman Rushdie, we'll just have to keep moving on. Get dressed, my darling, and then we'll go over and tell Rupert. We'll have to tell Captain Patricia as well.'

Nicholas got up from the table and took Charlotte's hands. He pulled her gently to her feet and then into his arms; they began to kiss. Charlotte put her arms round his neck and their kisses became more passionate. She unbuttoned Nicholas's pyjama top and slipped it off him, she covered his shoulders with kisses – no longer was she trembling with fear, but with pent-up desire. Nicholas could feel her hardened nipples through her shirt, and he began to unbutton it. Although it had been plain to them that they had been in love for many months, he had refrained from physically expressing it, and in the act of unbuttoning her shirt he remembered Theo saying that Charlotte was beautiful, but 'buttoned up' – he was well and truly overcoming that problem. He had restrained himself in the past, as once she had pushed him away saying she was awaiting a man she knew she would marry. Later she had apologised, but with difficulty explained that she had been damaged as a teenager by someone she thought she loved. She subsequently discovered he was just a philanderer, but the experience had scarred her. That morning she did not resist, her shirt fell to the ground. Her beauty took Nicholas's breath away; he poured out a stream of loving words and drew her to him. He told her he could not live without her and whispered, 'Please will you marry me?'

In answer, she pulled the cord on his pyjama trousers, saying, 'I think you can take this as an affirmative … ' and laughing, slipped out of her skirt. They began to kiss again, exploring each other's bodies. This moment 'out of time' was cruelly destroyed by the telephone extension from the house, shrilly ringing and bringing them back to their terror-filled world. They moaned in disbelief. Nicholas tried to continue kissing Charlotte, but she pushed him away saying, 'Paradise postponed, my darling.'

Nicholas picked up the phone. It was his hostess telling them that breakfast awaited them but the Army and the cadets would arrive in half an hour, so could they hurry over. Charlotte, who had overheard, said, 'I think we both need a quick shower first.'

Nicholas was just about to follow her when there was a loud knock on the door; he quickly put on his pyjama trousers. He found Charlotte's young brother-in-law, Sebastian, standing there looking embarrassed.

'Sorry to chase you but Mum's in a sweat about getting breakfast cleared as soon as possible, and Dad wants to speak to you urgently.'

Nicholas tried to look friendly and said they would be

right over. Charlotte had overheard this exchange and when Nicholas joined her she was already dressed. He himself quickly showered and in five minutes they both went over to the main house. In the dining room they found Rupert pacing up and down in a state of agitation. He stopped as they appeared, helped himself to a cup of coffee and sat down opposite them when they had made their choices of breakfast from the sideboard. He looked straight at them.

'Our postman has just been and when I'm around I usually have a gossip with him; he gave me some news which is rather alarming, as I feel it may be a threat to you. He told me he had just passed three large cars parked at the top of the road leading to the Helmsley main road. These cars were unloading a party of guns looking like comic opera Bavarians – large men in lederhosen wearing Bavarian jackets and ridiculous hats with feathers in them. What startled him, and me, is that he described the guns as having formidable telescopic sights, not your usual shotgun party. He also told me that when he drops the post at the Black Swan, he usually has a word with the manager. When he arrived at the hotel this morning, these Huns were gathering outside the hotel. The manager told him they were a pain in the neck, singing and drinking until the early hours, but on arrival, their English organiser had asked his receptionist to pinpoint, on a map, the exact location of Fortesque Hall.' Rupert snorted, 'He evidently told the manager that they had been asked by the Forestry Commission to come as an expert shooting party to cull deer which were getting out of hand up here. A likely story! I tell you, there'll be no Huns shooting on my land, but turning away such a powerfully gunned group is going to need outside assistance, so thank God the Army are coming in the next half hour.'

Both Nicholas and Charlotte had been looking forward to their breakfast, but their appetites disappeared with this news. Noticing their alarm, Rupert continued, 'I suggest you stay out of sight until the Army comes. I think we'll need the police involved as well. I'm very pally with our local Superintendent and suggest he finds fault with their passports. On the second floor, I have a small historic library and I suggest we go there after breakfast. It has the advantage of a hidden priest hole behind one of the shelves; you can hide in there if the enemy are so obsessed with destroying you. I think I can hear the newspaper man arriving now. I'll ask if he's seen anything of interest. You two tuck in to your breakfast.'

He reappeared looking disturbed.

'I've got the newspapers and also further information. The delivery man told me he saw the Boche climbing up on to the moors overlooking us and spreading out in a line on the escarpment. I think we should get up to the library right now. Bring your coffee and toast. I'll open up the priest hole so that if they attack the house, you'll be safe there.' All the time he spoke calmly, as if setting out plans for visiting a nearby stately home and indeed, they suspected he was enjoying the excitement.

With the newspapers under his arm, he took them up to the library. This was a charming room with old oak shelves on three walls and on the fourth, latticed windows with a view up the hill to the moors. Rupert went to a shelf and removed a large dictionary, behind which he pressed a button. The shelf swung inwards. He put the dictionary back on the shelf.

'Once you're inside, just shut the door. You'll find a release catch when you want to come out.' They peered inside and saw a couple of easy chairs, a table with candles on it, and a small fireplace on the far wall, over which hung a crucifix. Rupert smiled. 'Plenty of air via the fireplace. Sometimes I come here to think my way through a problem. St Robert Southall, the martyr, is reported to have hidden here, so I think a quiet word with him could be a help.'

Nicholas replied, 'I'm afraid the first words must be with our War Office contact. I suspect a discussion with your visiting Major will be a priority.' He rang Captain Patricia and told her of their discovery by Malplaquet, followed by the arrival of the threatening shooting party. However, he told her that the fact that the Army was about to arrive could be more than fortuitous.

Patricia told him he could brief the Major about to arrive, but only as far as their being under threat of assassination was concerned. He was also to get the Major to ring her immediately. She added that she had nothing to report from Switzerland. What she did not tell him was that she had lost touch with Brigadier Jackson, which was of increasing concern to her.

Having finished his call, Nicholas looked out of his window. His flesh froze; across the moor he saw six of the Teutonic Knights appearing over the brow of the moor carrying their guns at the ready. Nicholas was reminded of photographs of First World War troops charging out of their trenches. On the rim of the escarpment, six more were spread out. He could only conclude that they were about to make a reckless attack on them all, leaving them dead before disappearing. He told Charlotte to get ready to hide in the priest's hole, and ran down the stairs to get the others. On reaching the hall, he saw the back of Rupert going out through the front door. He was about to scream his name to warn him, but it was unnecessary – the cavalry had arrived.

He followed Rupert out of the door and saw two armoured cars and two lorries filled with soldiers, parking in front of the house. As they did so, a staff car arrived and, stopping before the door, deposited a Major in combat gear. Rupert was warmly shaking hands with the Major when Nicholas ran up to them and pointed to the six figures descending the hill towards them. As he pointed, the six men had stopped and were now kneeling, aiming their rifles towards the house.

Rupert grasped the situation but languidly turned to the Major.

'Charles, this is Nicholas. We have a little excitement laid on for you. He's under the protection of the War Office, being threatened by assassination. I think we should get inside quickly as those Huns you can see kneeling down on the hill are out to kill him.'

The Major made an expression of astonishment as he took in the sight of the six men, who were now advancing slowly. He shouted to the nearest armoured car, 'Patrick!' A head appeared out of the armoured car. The Major barked some orders to break open the live ammunition that they were carrying to use the next day on proper Army manoeuvres. He added that that included loading the armoured cars' machine guns. The Major walked to his staff car and told the driver to go back to the main road and stop the expected buses of school Army cadets descending to the house. As he was giving these orders, there were six flashes from the top of the moor. The tyres of the lorries and the staff car were shot to pieces, but the staff car was only hit on one side. It leant drunkenly over. There was the sound of escaping air.

'Bloody hell,' said the Major, 'they must assume we don't have any live ammunition. They must be mad as hatters.' He shouted again, 'Patrick, straddle the six coming down the hill. I'm going to order them to drop their guns. Every time they move, shoot the ground by their feet; if they carry on, shoot them in the legs. Tell Lieutenant Miles to take his armoured car back to the main road to stop any cadets coming down; our car's kaput. But first you come over here; I want your loudhailer.'

When he reached him, Lieutenant Patrick popped up with the loudhailer and handed it down to the Major. As he did so, there was the sound of firing from the top of the hill, and a loud ping as a bullet hit the side of the armoured car.

With the loudhailer in his hand, the Major wasted no time and ran in a zigzag manner back to the front door of the house and entered the hall to be greeted by the amazed occupants. He took off his beret and wiped his brow with a red handkerchief.

'Good training for Iraq; they're acting like a mad suicide squad.' He went back to the half-open front door and switched on the loudhailer, holding it so that it was half round the side of the door. They heard the armoured cars moving off and the sound of the soldiers from the lorries running over the gravel. The Major began to speak through the hailer.

'Lay down your arms and stand where you are … ' He was about to add another sentence, but the protruding end of the loudhailer was hit by a bullet and wrenched from his grasp. The Major had to admit to himself that it was an amazingly good shot as he retreated back into the house.

Rupert had taken the others up to the library, but they were cautiously peering through the cracks between the closed shutters. They could see Lieutenant Patrick's armoured car labouring up the hill in front of the house. The six assassins had taken cover in a line of grouse butts near the top of the hill to which they had retreated. The other armoured car was seen at the top of the moor travelling along the escarpment to where the other gunmen had been seen. Suddenly two of them stood up with anti-tank mortars hugging their shoulders, thoughtfully provided by Malplaquet in the limousines which had travelled with him from Temple Guiting. Two whooshing sounds followed the firing of these mortars, one to the armoured car on the top of the moor and the other to the one climbing the hill; both cars were enveloped in flames. The Teutonic Knights sheltering in the grouse butts belted to the top of the hill and disappeared. Five minutes later, a large helicopter was seen landing over the escarpment. It flew off almost immediately. The occupants of the armoured cars had managed to scramble out, but the blackened vehicles were wrecked.

The Major had witnessed this amazing débâcle and was no longer the calm man of action who had first appeared on the scene.

He turned to Rupert. 'What the hell has been going on here? You've landed me in the most ferocious military action seen in the UK within living memory!' He turned to look keenly at Nicholas. 'You must be a threat to one hell of an organisation.'

Nicholas nodded. 'You can say that again, but we are also a threat to Rupert and his family, so the sooner we move on the better.'

The Major regained his calm and said that first he would have to make a lot of phone calls, but he was sure they would be well protected. Nicholas suggested that when the Major was ready he should talk to Captain Patricia in the War Office. She could tell him the background to the day's happenings. He gave the Major her War Office telephone number and as the Major left the room he said he would make it his first call.

Soon after there was the sound of buses arriving so Rupert and the others left the library to greet the cadets, leaving Nicholas and Charlotte to enjoy some further stolen kisses. Once again they were interrupted, Rupert appearing with a Benedictine monk.

'This is Father Ambrose from Ampleforth. He makes his excuse to come every year for these manoeuvres so that we can enjoy a gossip; we usually come up here to have a coffee and brandy, then I leave him to commune with St Robert Southall, while I prepare the drinks for the party.'

Father Ambrose was a striking figure, tall and elegant with well-groomed, white hair. He had a lean energy about him. He gave them a firm handshake and looked at them intently after he sat down. He expressed warm concern for Nicholas and Charlotte, as Rupert had briefed him about the horrific attack of that morning and had informed him that a cultish organisation was responsible.

Sebastian appeared with coffee and Rupert opened a cupboard at the bottom of one of the bookshelves and produced a bottle of brandy and glasses. They sat round a table and tried to make sense of the morning; they agreed it was providential that it was the day of the annual manoeuvres and that it must have been a surprise for the enemy when they discovered the Army had live ammunition. Rupert told them that the police had been informed and, together with the Army, he hoped the attackers would be apprehended as soon as possible, as it should be an easy task to trace the helicopter that had arrived on the scene.

Father Ambrose added, 'You two young people must feel emotionally shattered, oppressed and depressed, I imagine.'

Nicholas immediately took to him. 'When I saw the enemy advancing down the hillside, I kept remembering the lines of a hymn we used to sing in Lent at school – *"Christian dost thou see them on the holy ground, how the troops of Midian prowl and prowl around"* and I thought to myself, here come the troops of Midian, and I was transported back to my school days as if I had sung it only yesterday. Funny that, like drowning people are said to see their lives flash before them.' Nicholas blushed, but his audience were in no way embarrassed. Charlotte moved her chair next to his and leant against him.

'How interesting … ' exclaimed Father Ambrose. 'Where were you at school?'

Nicholas smiled. 'I'm afraid I'm an outsider among you Papists. Melbury College, and lucky enough to progress to our jointly founded Michaelhouse at Cambridge.'

Charlotte laughed. 'Not an outsider – a high Anglican burning more incense than the Pope; eccentric relation I

151

should say. When the C of E appoints its first English woman bishop, I'm sure Nick will come rushing through our door with all the Anglo Catholic misogynist priests.'

Nicholas looked peeved. 'You speak nonsense, you hussy … '

They all laughed and Rupert knocked back his glass of brandy.

Charlotte's tone changed. 'Father, apart from the wickedness today, Nicholas and I and two American colleagues have had revealed to us tangible evil difficult to comprehend. We have been together for the last few weeks in Switzerland doing research for an organisation of bogus Templars. We discovered we were over a hidden volcano of evil and since it erupted I've tried to fathom out how the people involved could have become entangled in it, superficially normal and charming as they are. My question is, is this type of evil the responsibility of those involved, or can we believe in a Satan influencing them?' This unexpected question struck a chord, like a lightning flash illuminating a room.

Father Ambrose put down his cup of coffee and studied Charlotte with interest, as if seeing her for the first time.

'You ask a big and profound question which has spawned generations of opinions, but I'm happy to give you a view which I think is consistent with our beliefs. We accept the existence of Satan and a lot of our Lord's ministry consisted in the casting out of demons; these are fallen spirits, but their power is limited by God. They can only influence us if we allow it. We are given the grace to resist them. Yet their influence is stronger where many have given way – one only has to think of the Nazis, the horrors of the Soviet gulags or of the Cambodian genocides. One can easily see diabolic power at work.'

Nicholas shivered; he was remembering that every Wednesday night the College had a service of Compline containing its warning line: *"The devil goeth about like a roaring lion seeking whom he may devour."*

Rupert poured himself another brandy and stared moodily into his glass. 'We have recent examples on our doorstep. Diabolic is the word I use to describe the horrors of abuse in the Irish and American Catholic Church – I mean, what happened inside the brains of these people? I feel polluted when I read about them – priests persuading themselves that they are not breaking their vows of chastity because no women were involved, or most foul of all, a report I read, that some regarded it as a perk of the job. I mean, Father, if that is not satanic, what is?'

Ambrose lowered his eyes. 'A triumph for Satan – we've all been tarnished.' He sat back in silence.

Nicholas suspected Father Ambrose was praying, and after a moment he broke the silence.

'I seem to remember,' said Nicholas, 'that Aquinas taught that as Being is good, evil which is opposed to good, just as darkness to light, cannot signify anything but an absence of good. The paradox of evil: *"it both is, and is not"*. It exists not as a positive thing, but as a privation.'

Charlotte leant against Nicholas again and whispered, 'That's my boy!'

Ambrose agreed. 'But if you have this privation it causes a lot of damage and if shared with lots of people, it takes on a force of its own. However, St Augustine was said to have shouted, "I am not out of my mind, I do not say God creates evil." '

Rupert stood up. 'I'm beginning to feel the privation of lack of food in my tum. Join me downstairs in a quarter of an hour while I arrange it. The existence of God and evil is a mystery … ' He burst out laughing. 'My son Sebastian is looking at me in astonishment at the profundity of my mind.' He left the room chuckling and shortly afterwards the others followed him down to stretch their legs in the garden.

The Major did not join them for lunch; he was engaged in extensive damage limitation to his Army career. The armoured cars managed to regain a creaking life after the help of engineers sent over from the Regiment. They were then put on to low loaders and swiftly removed from the scene. When the Army cadets eventually arrived they were told that they had been held back as the Army had been having a live ammunition exercise, as they would shortly be leaving for Iraq.

Shortly after lunch, two police cars arrived at Fortesque Hall, lights flashing and sirens blaring. They then followed the Major in his staff car to examine the moor. Cartridges were found and the remains of mortar shells and the tyre marks of the helicopter were carefully measured.

When they returned, the Major asked Rupert if they could use the upper library as the police wanted to question Nicholas and Charlotte. A further police car would be coming soon with the manager of the Black Swan Hotel in Helmsley where the assassins had stayed. He asked Nicholas and Charlotte to join them. As they left the dining room, Father Ambrose came over and shook their hands warmly. He told them that, with Rupert, he had discussed their continuing safety. He understood that the Major had promised to mount guard over the house that night, but that obviously they would have to move on. He had considered the possibility of hiding them among the staff at Ampleforth College, but their enemies seemed clever at tracking them down and so that would not be possible as they could not risk the lives of school members. However, he thought it possible that the Abbot would agree to them staying a short while in an isolated cottage they owned on the edge of the moor, the other side of Hawnby. It was hidden away beyond a farm and could only be reached by a footpath. It was used occasionally as a hermitage for his brethren who wished to commune with God alone.

Charlotte thanked him very much but said their next move would have to be with the agreement of their contact in the

War Office, but they would bear it in mind. 'I hope to see you again,' said Father Ambrose. 'I've enjoyed our discussion. I will be getting my brethren all to pray for your safety and for the defeat of your enemy.' He smiled shyly and made a small sign of blessing over them both. As they climbed the stairs to the library, he stood watching them and gave them a final wave.

There they found Rupert, the Major and a posse of police, plus the hotel manager awaiting them. They wanted to hear what they knew about their attackers; the Major had explained that the Secret Service knew all the background but that Nicholas and Charlotte could give them their suspicions about the identity of the attackers. Nicholas then told them about Malplaquet, who he believed had been prowling about his cottage the night before, and that from the bizarre Bavarian appearance of their attackers, he suspected they were part of a German cult. He gave them Malplaquet's Temple Guiting address.

They then asked the hotel manager to repeat his description of the shooting party. He told them that the Englishman organising the shoot called himself Samuel Connaught and his chauffeur, Mr Fred Frost. He said Mr Connaught had white hair, but thinking back, he remembered it had looked suspiciously like a wig. His chauffeur was thick set, looked tough and wore dark glasses all the time. When they had arrived at the hotel, Mr Connaught had given him a list of the names of the Germans. The hotel manager looked at his register which he had brought with him and read out the names, 'Weber – Schubert – Mahler – Bach – Schroder – Warburg – Kleinwort.'

Before he could finish, Rupert burst out laughing, 'An amazing collection of names of famous German composers and merchant bankers!'

The police superintendent looked embarrassed. The hotel manager continued telling them that Mr Connaught had checked out the whole party early that morning, saying that they had to leave unexpectedly due to his German friends having a credit crisis in their German company. He had paid in cash and for the cancelled night as well. The only other thing he remembered was that their cars all had German number plates, even though they had right-hand drive. The police superintendent thanked the manager and announced that they would immediately activate a possible arrest of Malplaquet when he returned to Temple Guiting. He added that they would want to know if there were any sightings of helicopters. He then turned to the Major and said, 'By the way, the helicopter that rescued the attackers was seen by your neighbour at Arden House, and he said it was an Army helicopter. Are you sure, Major, this wasn't an exercise that just got out of control?'

The Major looked dumbfounded. 'An Army helicopter! That's just not possible.'

The police superintendent looked smug after delivering this bombshell, and said they would leave with the manager to see if they could find any fingerprints in the so-called Mr Connaught's room at the hotel.

When the police had left, the Major suggested that they make contact with Captain Patricia and wondered whether there was a speaker phone in the house that they could use so they could all join in the conversation. Rupert said he had one in his office. Once there, Rupert sat himself down. Top secret or not, he was not going to miss any further excitement.

They got through to Patricia and the Major gave her the latest news and told her that the police were now involved. He also told her a local witness had claimed that the helicopter which effected the escape of the enemy was an Army one. Patricia expressed astonishment but said she would immediately get records of any Army helicopter movements that day. She went on to say that she would have to find another safe house for Nicholas and Charlotte. She added that the Templars seemed to be working on inside information, not only evidenced by the attack on Fortesque Hall, but also on Theo and Kirsten in America; she had just heard about them from the CIA. She would contact them next morning and a car with security personnel would come to Yorkshire to escort them to their new quarters.

As they finished the call, the Major looked out of the window and saw a platoon of cadets running past the house towards the woods at the back. The Major excused himself and said he must now join the cadets as an adjudicator, hopefully less stressful than the start of the day.

Left alone, they sat quietly for a while, trying to absorb the reality that they could all have been killed. Nicholas broke the silence.

'Rupert, I understand from Sebastian that he had come home to borrow a car so that he could pick up a girlfriend living near Stow-on-the-Wold, en route to a college ball at Merton.'

Rupert nodded. 'I would even have lent him my vintage Bentley to help him develop a love life and hopefully postpone his Benedictine novice ambitions until he is more mature – why do you mention it?'

Nicholas took a deep breath. 'Can I ask him to deliver a letter to the Grand Master of the English Templars, de Malplaquet. Their HQ is very close to Stow. You see I happen to have some blank, headed notepaper I filched from the office of the Grand Master of the Order in Switzerland. For some time I've had a handwritten invitation from him and I'm quite a good forger and able to copy his writing. I thought I could send a forged letter ordering him to Switzerland and calling off his murderous attacks – that would give us a few days' peace. When he arrives unannounced in Switzerland that should also cause some confusion.' He went on to explain the arcane manner in which the Grand Master communicated and asked Rupert if he had any sealing wax, as he had a ring similar to the one used by the Grand Master in sealing his letters.

Rupert looked at him admiringly. 'I'll ask Sebastian immediately. This is proving one hell of an adventure.' He left them again singing, 'I am an Admiral of the Queen's Navy … '

Charlotte went over to Nicholas and perched on his lap and began kissing him. Once again they were frustrated; Nicholas's own mobile phone rang. It was his friend Francis, the Chaplain of Michaelhouse; he sounded pleased with himself.

'You remember the Armenian letter you gave me to see if I could get it translated? Some weeks ago, I took it to a priest I know in the Armenian Church in Iverna Gardens, London. He's just got back to me.'

Nicholas immediately pressed the speaker on his phone so that Charlotte could hear. 'That's brilliant, Francis, what did it say?'

Francis replied, 'I'll just put my spectacles on … ' There was a rustle of paper. Nicholas and Charlotte leant towards the phone, tense with curiosity. 'It reads, "*You are commanded to officiate at the Supreme Sacrifice in the Temple of Zurzach, Midsummer's Day, 4pm.*" This is a typed invitation; underneath in a calligrapher's hand is a note saying, "*This sacrifice will ensure our Jerusalem triumph, which will start at the same time.*" By the way, my Armenian contact had the envelope with it, addressed to Bishop Krasnos. He wanted to know how I had come by this as he's very much persona non grata in the Armenian Church, recently defrocked for being involved in a scandalous black mass. I must say, Nicholas, you seem to be moving in exotic circles. What on earth is this about?'

Nicholas gripped the phone. 'I'll tell you all about it next time I see you, but could you just confirm that it's about a sacrifice to take place at four o'clock on Midsummer's Day to ensure the success of a simultaneous happening in Jerusalem? This is the most important news. Thank you, Francis.' Before finishing, they had a brief further conversation about the mood of Canon Frobisher, the Master, which had been aggravated by Francis successfully having had published a spoof letter in the *News Chronicle* which was publicly ridiculing Canon Frobisher within the University. He told Nicholas to buy it and read it so that they could discuss it later, adding that his attack was proving a riotous success. Nicholas shook his head as he put down the phone.

Charlotte stood up and said that they must ring Captain Patricia immediately. Midsummer's Day was the day after tomorrow. When they got through to Captain Patricia, her voice was subdued and weary. Before they could speak she told them that she had further alarming news. She had concluded that she would move them to share the closely guarded safe house, where Sergeant Maggie was living. She had received reports that Maggie was bored and restless, and she thought that their company could help her as well as providing them with protection. She had just rung the officer in charge of the house to be told that ten minutes ago, they had found her strangled in her bedroom. Evidently she had been walking in the garden, talking to one of the guards, when the gate bell rang. This gate was in a high wall that shut off the drive to the main road. The guard went to the sentry box and saw, on a security camera monitor, two Indian women, carrying a load of saris over their arms. They announced over the intercom that they were offering these at bargain prices. Maggie had heard this and, to relieve her boredom, asked if they could be let in. The guard agreed but stayed in his box reading his newspaper, while Maggie went into the house with the Indians to try on the saris. Ten minutes later the Indians left, saying the lady was very happy with the saris she bought and thanking the guard warmly. Later the guard commented that a sari wrapped around the head of the taller of the two women, had slipped, revealing a prominent Adam's apple. He had gone into the house half an hour later to have a cup of coffee with Maggie, which was their daily custom. She was not downstairs and, calling out, he got no reply, so he went upstairs to her bedroom, which he found locked. Assuming she was trying on her new saris, he had made himself a cup of coffee and it was only when she had not appeared before lunch that he had called the duty officer. On breaking down the door, they found her dead, strangled by a silk rope with a running knot.

Wide-eyed with horror, Nicholas exclaimed, 'My God, Patricia, they've got the Thugs in the country as well as the Teutonic Knights.'

Captain Patricia replied, 'Now you know why I am so anxious about your security.'

Nicholas then told her about the letter addressed to Bishop Krasnos and that they had just received the translation. It seemed to them that unless the whole operation had been closed down in Switzerland, there was the likelihood that in two days' time they could be faced with the horror of the destruction of the Dome of the Rock in Jerusalem. Nicholas asked whether the Templars in Switzerland had been arrested yet.

Captain Patricia replied, 'As far as I know it should all be completed in the next twenty-four hours. Take the greatest care and I will find another safe house before the car comes for you tomorrow morning.'

As Nicholas discussed with Charlotte the horror of Maggie's death, they wondered aloud whether they themselves would escape; the Templars seemed relentless in their attempts to destroy them as witnesses to their inner secrets. They wondered why it had taken so long for the Swiss operation to be closed down, even though the death of Colonel Baker might have delayed matters for twenty-four hours.

This question was also exercising Captain Patricia. She had heard from Brigadier Jackson that he had alerted the authorities in Switzerland, but he had been elusive and she had discovered that he had not been in places that he had told her he was going to. He had never appeared at the horse trials as a judge. He also told her that he had to make a visit to Sandhurst, and needing to contact him she had tried to ring him there, only to be told that Sandhurst had no knowledge of an intended visit by him. While she was awaiting reports on helicopter movements, she had rung the Defence Attaché in the British Embassy in Berne; Brigadier Jackson said he had set up a meeting there with Swiss security. She felt an increasing unease when the Attaché said the Brigadier never contacted him. She then got the report on helicopter movements that morning: the only one had been a flight from the Military Academy at Shrivenham. A Brigadier Jackson had been a passenger with a pilot he had brought with him. He had said they wanted to test its suitability for security work. When the helicopter returned, the Brigadier kept the flight plan. A quarter of an hour later, Patricia received radar reports of a helicopter over the Yorkshire moors and later tracked it to a hill in the Cotswolds near Moreton-in-Marsh, a few minutes from the mainline station. Most trains leaving Moreton stopped at Reading from where taxis or buses could take passengers to Heathrow. It was also near to the Templar HQ.

Captain Patricia felt sick with fear, for if Brigadier Jackson was an associate of the Templars everything fell into place, and if he was assisted also by someone in their sector, the killing of Colonel Baker and the knowledge of the address of Sergeant Maggie's safe house would have been possible with inside help. Captain Patricia feverishly typed her conclusions and requested a meeting with Lieutenant General Maitland, head of MI6-66. She was granted an interview within the hour.

While she waited, she heard from the Major at Fortesque Hall. The police had contacted him to say they had drawn a blank at the Temple Guiting HQ. They had found Malplaquet tending his bees and had been led to him by a housekeeper who told them he had been there all day and the day before. She had called over a nearby gardener, who had corroborated her story. In addition the Helmsley police had reported that there were no suspicious fingerprints to be found in the room he had occupied.

Captain Patricia reflected that a minor war had erupted that morning in an English national park, but the participants had evaporated into thin air. Just before she was about to see Lieutenant General Maitland, Nicholas rang her and gave her the information about the translation of the letter to Bishop Krasnos. She gave him the news that Brigadier Jackson would be replaced by a higher officer. She told him that no further discussion should take place with him. The information about the letter would be passed on to Israeli intelligence. She also told him that she had heard from the CIA that there had been an attempt to attack Theo and Kirsten. She confirmed that a car would still be sent to Yorkshire to collect them the next morning and take them to their new safe house.

Nicholas told Charlotte what he had just learnt from Captain Patricia, and thought they should ring Theo to learn more about the attack they had suffered. When they got through, Theo told them they had been moved to a new location on Martha's Vineyard. He told them they were in a lovely house with sea views, but if they left it, they had to get clearance from one of the security guards. He explained that the attack on their first house had been horrendous; it was attacked by two men with sub-machine guns who tried to smash through a French window. Fortunately the window was made of bullet-proof glass and even more fortunately, one of their guards leant out of an upstairs window to smoke a cigarette and, on seeing them, used his machine pistol to shoot the attackers stone dead. 'Very Al Capone!'

Nicholas briefly described their own ordeal, and then gave Theo the information about the timing of the Jerusalem attack to coincide with the ritual that was to take place in the Templar Castle. This news was received by a long silence and then Theo exclaimed, 'Holy cow, that gives us screamingly little time! I spoke to that Professor Mahoud, the one we met at the seminar in Zurich, to see whether he could make sense of the words I heard in the Templar crypt, hoping that he might recognise where the bombing helicopter would land. I'll ring him again now and see whether he's been successful. Keep your phone on; we must talk again as soon as I've spoken to him. The names came back to me after I woke from a dream about Jerusalem – *Shaar Zion* and then separately the word *Shalom,* but of course that's such an overused Jewish word mixed into my dream, I suppose.'

Ten minutes later Theo rang back, full of excitement. He said, 'Our Prof is sure *Shaar Zion* is the Zion Gate which leads to the Armenian quarter; also on nearby open ground there's a ring road called *Ha Shalom.* He's one hundred per cent certain and it makes sense that they should have chosen that spot as three Armenian priests coming out from the Armenian quarter would not cause any comment, just as Karl said in the crypt. The Prof is insisting we get out there to Jerusalem by tomorrow night so that we can convince the Israeli authorities. He says they won't listen to a Muslim professor, probably dismissing it as a diversion from a possible Hamas attack, adding that he was known to have connections with that organisation. Our evidence may be more believable when Kirsten confirms her Jewish connections. We have made up our minds and if we can get away from Martha's Vineyard we can catch an overnight flight from Boston to pick up a connection in Europe to Tel Aviv. Can you both come – please?'

'Hang on,' said Nicholas as he relayed the news to Charlotte; she nodded vigorously. Nicholas confirmed they would do their best to get there, and that he had the Professor's phone number so that he would contact him to let him know they were on their way. Obviously they couldn't tell MI6 or the CIA in case they were imprisoned in their safe houses for their own safety.

Nicholas and Charlotte hugged each other in excitement. Once again they were interrupted as Rupert and his son entered and told them that the forged letter to Malplaquet would be delivered with pleasure, a small way of registering disapproval of their family home being pockmarked by high-velocity bullets. Nicholas said he would write it at once. He wrote it in the format used by the Grand Master when inviting them to the Templar Castle.

He wrote, *'Report to the Grand Master of the Temple of the Holy Sepulchre, Zurzach, immediately. Postpone further attacks, your lack of success must be explained. Our messenger will await your immediate reply.'*

Nicholas judged it to be a good forgery and hoped that Malplaquet would accept it, as he must be under considerable stress. Nicholas addressed the envelope and took the letter down to Rupert to show them. Rupert provided the sealing wax and Nicholas imprinted on it his Templar ring seal.

Rupert said, 'That should cure any constipation problem.'
Sebastian just smiled and took the letter.

Meanwhile Charlotte discovered they could get a plane that evening from Hull to Amsterdam with a connection the next morning to Tel Aviv. In order to slip away from the guards who had been assigned to them, they decided they would have to ask Rupert to help. They went to find him and were surprised by his reaction to their request.

Rupert paced up and down in front of them, gazing at the floor, murmuring, 'Jerusalem the golden, with milk and honey blessed,' then he looked up. 'Charlotte, I don't think I ever told your sister, Sarah, but for part of my life I was a regular officer in the Blues and Royals – I got a bit fed up with the ceremonial farting about and the Army kindly made me Military Attaché in Jerusalem for my last five years. Very interesting billet, I can tell you. I made a lot of friends.' Rupert began to speak quickly. 'One of them became a particularly good friend, an Israeli General. I even invited him here to shoot grouse. Not very successfully, he only shot a brace. As you know, grouse go like the clappers so shooting that brace became the most exciting shoot he had ever done; you know, both barrels – one – two, and then dropping right by his butt. Ever since then he's asked me to return to Jerusalem and stay with him. Your Arab Professor friend and your connection with him might be a handicap if we are seeking Israeli help. I think my General friend will believe your unbelievable story if you have me with you. I'm volunteering to be your liaison officer and help you get away. We'll drive to Hull this evening with you both under a blanket in the back of my estate car. My wife can host the post-manoeuvres party. What do you say?'

Charlotte said later that Sir Rupert was like an eager gun dog, straining to get in on the kill. They accepted his help with enthusiasm, realising his Israeli connections could be invaluable. Rupert gave them the use of his debit card to get all three tickets on line and said that he would arrange a hotel for them that night in Amsterdam. He said, 'I know a super one, the Amstel; I used to go there for R and R when I was stationed in Hanover. I'll get on to it right now. I suggest you put your feet up; it's going to be a busy day or two ahead of us.'

18

Nicholas and Charlotte agreed they would speak to Captain Patricia to say that they had friends abroad where they would be safe and that they would keep in touch daily. Nicholas rang Theo and told him they were on their way to Jerusalem with Rupert and told him about Rupert's military connections in Israel and they would hope to meet him, Theo, at the Professor's house the next evening. Theo confirmed that the Professor was in the picture, and that they had managed to get to the airport on Martha's Vineyard where Kirsten had charmed a millionaire into giving them a lift to Boston in his private plane.

Later that afternoon Rupert appeared in his estate car and, checking that the coast was clear, Nicholas and Charlotte got into the back and were covered by two rugs, smelling strongly of dogs. Rupert said once they were clear of Helmsley, they could join him in the front. Rupert's wife came to see them off and expressed anxiety about their safety and her own, saying, 'Tell me, Rupert, where can I go to be safe while you are away, apart from the secret library room?'

Rupert, wanting to be off on his adventure, patted her on the shoulder and said, 'Just get into a state of grace, and stay there, otherwise I know any of our friends and relations will welcome you. I'll keep in touch.' He leapt in the car, revved the engine and zoomed off.

An hour later they reached the Humber Bridge, once Europe's longest single-span suspension bridge, an electoral bribe by the Socialist minister, Barbara Castle, to the voters on both sides of the bridge. Nevertheless Rupert called for 'Three cheers for Barbara Castle – her multi-million bribe is getting us to the airport to save the world!'

There were no problems going through passport control and it was a relief for them to be travelling with a purpose rather than hiding away in some safe house. Before boarding the plane Nicholas bought the *News Chronicle*. The Chaplain's letter was farcical. It read:

Regent's Park
19 June

Sir – Yesterday the Honourable Judge Charles Withers sentenced a drunken gang of yobs in Newcastle Crown Court and remarked that they had behaved like stupid baboons.

Stupid we are not, and my acceptance of a place at Michaelhouse, Cambridge, is proof of this. Having gained first-class honours at the Department of Experimental Psychology my acceptance was solely by interview with the Master, Canon Frobisher.

Canon Frobisher and I are now good friends; he says my voice synthesiser reminds him of Professor Hawkins but this will not prevent me from taking Holy Orders. As I am already a Primate, I shall be the first lady bishop of the Church of England in the United Kingdom.

Canon Frobisher is a sweety and I can reveal that behind his 'Affirming Catholicism' façade, he is a crypto-Evangelical and a secret supporter of CICU. Yours with a swing

Babs Boon

PS Some of my relations are visiting Newcastle with the circus and I must warn the Honourable Judge they intend to 'put his lights out'.

Nicholas was surprised that this had been published, though later it was revealed that the letters editor of the newspaper had been away sick and that an intern had let it slip through. Nicholas knew the Master would use every endeavour to discover who was the writer and feared that as he was known to be a close friend of the Chaplain, he might be suspected.

When they arrived at Schipol Airport, Rupert was in an ebullient mood, which continued to express itself as he announced in the taxi to the hotel in Amsterdam, 'Twenty-five years ago, I had a lovely frustrated Dutch lady friend, so in the R and R department I had little rest but a hell of a lot of recreation.' For the rest of the journey, he looked out of the window, silently remembering another era.

The Amstel Hotel lived up to their expectations. They dined well in the hotel restaurant at water level, looking out over a wide canal where both large commercial barges and pleasure boats glided past decorated house boats moored opposite. At the end of their meal, the head waiter came over and pointed to a smart motor launch coming alongside the hotel landing stage.

'That's the launch you ordered, sir, but we'll wait until you've finished. Plenty of time for coffee, cigars and liqueurs.' Rupert had organised this private canal tour, to end their evening before their early departure next day to Tel Aviv.

Charlotte clapped her hands. 'Rupert, you are spoiling us ... ' Then she whispered to Nicholas, 'Can we tell him our news?'

The news of their engagement was received with exclamations of happiness and congratulations. As they boarded the boat a waiter appeared with a bottle of champagne and glasses. This resulted in the memory of the details of their boat trip being somewhat blurred, though they remembered Rupert's expressions of disgust as they passed various garish clubs and windows occupied by semi-naked women of the night. Charlotte's eyes widened with amazement; she had never been to Holland before. When they returned to the hotel at the end of their tour, they refused offers of further refreshment and went to bed.

Nicholas and Charlotte had adjoining rooms. They were both restless for each other and sleep eluded them, not helped by the erotic visions they had passed. The phone rang in Nicholas's room. It was Charlotte, 'I can't sleep and I'm frightened.'

Nicholas replied, 'I think I know a cure,' and a minute later joined her. They recalled Rupert's remark in the taxi, 'no rest but plenty of recreation.'

Next day they had to endure the intense procedure exercised by El Al security: there was no question of their bags being checked in and sent straight to the plane; instead they went to a separate departure area where every item was minutely examined. Next to them a woman with a mass of gift-wrapped presents was reduced to tears as each one was unwrapped and analysed. They were travelling with an airline that pragmatically knew its country was at war.

Their flight was uneventful and having landed on time in Tel Aviv and again survived the gauntlet of security checks, Rupert insisted they took a taxi directly to travel the thirty-five miles to Jerusalem instead of the airline buses. Neither Nicholas nor Charlotte had ever been to Israel. The highway from Tel Aviv to Jerusalem is all uphill and en route they entered the Jezreel valley. There the taxi driver pointed out the ruins of the fortress city of Megiddo, where King Solomon had built stables. Rupert added that biblical scholars believed the final battle between good and evil would take place there, the Apocalypse of Armageddon. As if to emphasise the possibility of this final battle, hulks of wrecked military vehicles could be seen, left as memorials to the convoys that forced their way through to Jerusalem during the Israeli War of Independence. These grim tokens were forgotten as the twisting road left the pink-tinted, rocky surroundings to part and reveal ahead of them the holy city of Jerusalem; the Dome of the Rock glistened in the fading sun. Nothing can prepare a reflective traveller for his first sight of Jerusalem: built on its mountain, it has existed for five thousand years and is the holy city of Jews, Christians and Muslims.

They had given the taxi driver the Professor's address and they made for the eastern side of the city, where the old city lies. Soon they were passing close to the massive walls of the Temple Mount, and then, they turned sharply left down a narrow road. All the while Rupert had been giving them a running commentary on the various sights and as they turned, exclaimed, 'We're going in at the Lion's Gate, through the city walls to the Via Dolorosa.'

Charlotte felt choked with the emotional impact of travelling where Christ had carried his cross. They found themselves in the Muslim quarter. Arab crowds milled along the street and their oriental music filled the air. A few minutes later they turned sharp right.

'This will take us up to Herod's Gate,' murmured Rupert.

The taxi driver remarked on his knowledge of the city and Rupert confessed to his five-year stint there. The driver moved slowly down the road, looking for the house of the Professor. Finally he sounded his horn in triumph – they had arrived.

19

At the same time as Professor Mahoud was receiving his guests in Jerusalem, the Templar Deputy Master, Karl, was checking into a bedroom at the Bauer au Lac Hotel in Zurich. Here he was to be joined by Lady Natasha. He was tired; they had spent several hours rehearsing the Supreme Ceremony planned for the following day. When Natasha arrived he ordered a bottle of champagne to be sent up to the room. Natasha was still beautiful, but had lost her air of arrogance after her ordeal in the coffin. In her waking hours she was obsessed with the need to know that the English and American academics had been eliminated. Indeed she had begged the Grand Master to have them kidnapped and flown back in a private plane to Zurzach so that they too could suffer the ordeal of the coffin, but speed was of the essence; it was necessary to kill them at once to remove them as witnesses against the Templar Order.

Her first words to Karl were to enquire whether or not they had been killed. She knew the attacks of the previous day had failed both in America and Yorkshire. Karl could only tell her of the elimination of Sergeant Margaret by the Thugs, but the failure of the other attempts could be a fatal threat to the existence of the Templars at Zurzach. Natasha raged at him, saying they should have left their elimination solely to the Thugs, instead of the ridiculous English Grand Master, Malplaquet.

'The idiot turned up here unannounced this afternoon, claiming GM had summoned him; if he has left evidence of his attempts to kill the English couple he'll implicate us to destruction. GM has put him in solitary for the time being, but I think he should be a candidate for burial – we need absolute obedience in the Order at this time. The last burial ritual attempt caused a weakening of discipline as well as my intolerable suffering.'

The mention of her near extinction caused her to burst into hysterical sobbing, and she flung herself face down on the bed and pounded the pillows with her fists. Karl tried to comfort her by saying that their Jerusalem triumph the next day would enable them to rise above any accusations; the world would be solely concerned with the threat of conflagration spreading from Jerusalem. The plans for UN status in Jerusalem would inevitably follow. Then they could look forward to taking possession of the Shroud of Turin. With that their future power would be boundless.

Natasha lay silent for a moment, then got up from the bed and seized the lapels of his black linen blazer. She began to shake him, speaking hysterically. 'What if those academics persuade the international police to move against us? Our English Templar, Brigadier Jackson, has merely been playing for time but should have assassinated Colonel Baker's assistant as well as blowing up his car en route to the airport. Everyone needs to be reminded what happens if they fail. We must also face the fact of what will happen to us: only GM knows where the Abbey of Sarmouz is, only he brings us monthly the elixir of life, so what will happen to us if he gets killed? You and the Council must persuade him to appoint substitutes with access to the Abbey and its elixir. I don't need to remind you of our real ages, and nobody knows whether we suddenly wither without the elixir or just die suddenly.'

She shook him again and moved her hands to his neck. He misunderstood her and pushed her back on to the bed and as he moved to join her, she slapped his face hard and slipped away from him, saying, 'Not today, not till this nightmare is over.' She went into the bathroom, and five minutes later, having washed away the ravages of her hysteria, left the room, slamming the door behind her.

Karl opened the champagne and drank two glasses in quick succession. He moodily reviewed the events of the afternoon rehearsal of the sacrificial ceremony, timed to coincide with the destruction of the Dome of the Rock in Jerusalem. In the rehearsal, a doll had been substituted for the intended victim – his very own child. He had nearly fainted when, at the climax, the Grand Master had slashed the doll's throat; it had been filled with red wine and it poured out into the basin-like depression on top of the altar stone. It dawned on Karl that for him there was no longer any sacred mystery or promise of spiritual powers; it was sordid and ridiculous. For days he had admitted to growing feelings of revulsion at the dark side of the cult: no further ecstasy or excitement beckoned, an emotional desert seemed to await him. His long life of debauchery and power had drained him and flung him on a barren shore. It was a defining moment.

20

In Jerusalem there was a mood of excitement and optimism in the house of Professor Mahoud, a mood boosted by his warm hospitality. A delicious spread of local delicacies awaited them with its central delight of a large dish of roasted pigeons. Although the Professor was a firm follower of the Prophet as regards alcohol, he did not deny it to his guests and they enjoyed chilled white Lebanese wine and mellow Israeli red.

The Professor sat with them and listened to their saga of the unfolding of events in the Templar Castle in Zurzack and their final escape. Before they had sat down to dinner, he and Theo had eliminated any alternatives to their conclusion as to where the helicopter would land to collect the disguised Templars and their bomb and it was agreed this would definitely take place near the Zion Gate.

Rupert had rung his Israeli General friend before leaving Amsterdam and had outlined the threat to the Dome of the Rock. It had been agreed he would ring the General when they reached the Professor's house and that the General would join them after dinner to finalise the action they would take against the Templar bombers.

At nine o'clock the General rang to confirm the Professor's address and was given the number and the name of the street – *El Qada Siva*. Shortly afterwards there was a loud knock on the front door which the Professor's wife went to open. The General, fully dressed in military uniform, bounced into the room full of energy. Charlotte and Kirsten thought he looked glamorous. He marched briskly over to Rupert. They hugged each other and to everyone's surprise began speaking to each other in Hebrew. They caught the words,

'*Shalom*', '*todaraba*', and '*sliha*', slipping effortlessly from Rupert's lips as he wished the General peace and thanked him very much for coming to help them and expressed his sorrow (*sliha*) for not coming back to Jerusalem before. He then introduced the General as 'Samuel' to everyone and the General shook all their hands, saying, 'Everyone calls me Sam.' He beamed especially at the Professor; they had met before. The Professor had helped to quieten a mob of Arab students, bent on rioting over a minor issue.

The General sat down next to Rupert, resting a hand affectionately on his shoulder, and accepted a glass of white wine. He sipped at it occasionally while they gave him the story of the Templars and how Nicholas and Theo had overheard the plans to bomb the Dome of the Rock and how they had later learnt of the timing of the attack and, with the help of the Professor, where it would start. Unfortunately they had only just had these final details.

It was understood that the bombers would be leaving the Zion Gate around 15.55 the following day, Midsummer's Day, to join a helicopter to take them to bomb the Dome at 16.00. He had deduced that this helicopter would land between the Gateway and the road, Ma' Ale Ha-Shalom.

The General took out a small notebook from his breast pocket and began to write the details. 'We Israelis also call it the Gate of the Prophet David – Bab Nabi Daud.' He took his hand off Rupert's shoulder and tapped the table gently. Everyone was silent, watching him. He looked up; his usual expression of bonhomie had vanished. 'There are two extremely dangerous sides to this threat. The first is local. Nicholas and Theo, you say you overheard that the enemy, let's call them that, would be armed with sub-machine guns and that one of them would be carrying a bomb. Thus there is great danger to innocent life if we try to apprehend them as they come out of the Bab Nabi Daud. It's very busy at that time of day and they will not be the only ones dressed

175

as Armenian priests. If they come out separately and get together only at the helicopter, it's going to be mighty difficult to spot who is a genuine Armenian priest, because their black cloaks and large hoods make a good and simple disguise. If we start a general search of every Armenian priest around, the enemy will see it happening as they come out of the Gate, so to get to the helicopter, they might rush out shooting. Obviously we shall shoot back and the bomb might be exploded; the loss of life will be horrific. My conclusion is that we should have disguised Army units around and we should wait to machine gun them to hell as they run towards the helicopter. Hopefully there will be no one near it because of the turbulence from the propellers. The second great danger is if they somehow succeed in destroying the Dome. Can we be sure that they don't have a plan to attack from another direction?'

Rupert interrupted. 'Unfortunately there have been previous attempts – all failed, thank God. In 1969 a nutty young Australian fundamentalist, one Dennis Rohan, set the Al-Aqsa Mosque on fire. Professor Mahoud no doubt can confirm the Jews got the blame from the Arab Commission because they were in control. The loony responsible said he was destroying Satan's temple and by doing so he would be made King of Jerusalem. Unfortunately this city has a horrible attraction and every year loonies come here convinced they are the Messiah.'

The General nodded. 'In 1982 the worst of the plots was masterminded by an explosives expert. He was with others, convinced the Messiah was about to arrive and the third Jewish temple would be built, but first the Dome of the Rock had to be destroyed. It was called off because they couldn't find a Rabbi to bless the attack. With the USA supporting us, and the Russians supporting the Palestinians at the time, it could have started World War Three. So if this plot succeeds tomorrow, who knows? Thank goodness you've overheard the threat and are coming to help us defeat it. We will meet again tomorrow at 15.00. By then we will have our plans in place and we can put everyone in the picture.'

Rupert had been invited to stay with the General and left with him at the conclusion of their meeting.

Next day the Professor had told them he would give them a tour of the city, which had the advantage of distracting them from the threat of the afternoon attack.

Rupert, having lived in Jerusalem, was spending the day with his friend General Sam and would meet up again as arranged at the Professor's house at three o'clock.

The following morning the Professor fuelled them with strong Turkish coffee before shepherding them out to start their tour. His house was close to the Temple Mount and so they started there. When they entered the top of the Temple Mount they found themselves in an area shaded with trees, beyond which the blue-tiled façade of the golden Dome rose before them. The Professor explained that the mosque contained the rock from which Muhammad ascended on a winged horse through the seven heavens with the Archangel Gabriel and met God before awaking back in Mecca; thus this spot is considered the third most holy in the world of Islam. Also Jewish tradition claims that the stone was the foundation on which the world was created and on which Abraham was prepared to sacrifice his son, Isaac. Over it the temples of Herod and Solomon were built and it was the location of the Holy of Holies. It was also the temple in which the prophet Jesus taught and drove out the traders. Hence it is the epicentre of the three monotheistic faiths.

Seeing it for the first time, the four pilgrims felt overwhelmed by its spiritual associations. Before them rose flights of steps and on either side stood arches built by the Crusaders. At the top, two fountains splashed where worshippers washed before prayers. Having admired the wonders of the interior of the Dome, the Professor then moved them on to the Al Aqsa Mosque. This was beyond the Dome directly over the Western Wailing Wall, sacred to the Jews. He explained it was so called because the Jews bewailed the destruction of the original temples. As they approached it, Theo told them that the Templars had used it as their headquarters when Jerusalem became controlled by the Crusaders. Here the first nine Templars were said to have excavated beneath it and to have discovered the treasures of the Holy Grail, the Shroud of Turin and even the Ark of the Covenant. With these relics came their phenomenal growth and wealth.

The interior of the Al Aqsa Mosque was floored with acres of sumptuous carpets and its ceiling gilded. The Professor told them this was the main place of Islamic prayer in Jerusalem and that one prayer there was said to be worth forty thousand elsewhere. They then descended from the top of the Temple Mount and walked down to the Wailing Wall, where Kirsten was able to make the traditional Jewish prayers. While she was doing this the others stood on the perimeter watching the scene. The Professor pointed out a large opening at one end of the Wall and told them that it led to Solomon's stables and that later they had been used by the Crusaders. Nicholas could not help thinking to himself that the men swaying back and forth at their prayers were exuberant in their devotions and totally foreign compared with the subdued worship in his College chapel. When Kirsten rejoined them the Professor announced that it was time for lunch and that they would therefore go to a café well known for its excellent kebabs. Refuelled, they would afterwards visit the Church of the Holy Sepulchre before returning to his house to meet up with Rupert and the General.

Nicholas bought a copy of an English guide to Jerusalem en route to the restaurant and, seated at their table, thumbed through it while they enjoyed a bottle of white wine before the arrival of their kebabs. He paused at a section on Mount Zion. He read that circling the mount was the Hirsom Valley, called Gehenna, meaning hell in the Bible. In Canaanite times it was sacred to the cult of Moloch. This unpleasant faith burnt children alive as sacrifices and fires were kept burning permanently for that purpose in the valley. Nicholas wished he had not read this, because it jolted him back to the threat of sacrifice planned by the Templars. It cast a pall over the joy they had experienced that morning. Charlotte noticed his change of mood; he passed the guidebook round the table, infecting them with similar feelings of depression. They explained this to Professor Mahoud and showed him the guidebook.

'Moloch, another manifestation of Shaytan,' he commented.

Nicholas told them of their discussion in Yorkshire about good and evil. Theo said he believed in the devil and that the Grand Master and his followers were probably possessed to some degree. He also believed that creation itself had later been evilly infected, hence death and disease. He felt satanic forces could have perverted aspects of creation, hence the malarial mosquito or the bilharzia worm, which attacks the liver. He finished by saying most of this was reflected in the doctrine of original sin.

The Professor shook his head. 'We Muslims do not believe that teaching. Mankind is certainly tested for heaven but in an Islamic society Sharia law will protect him. Evil is certainly not equal to good.'

The discussion continued throughout the meal and the Professor corrected many misconceptions about Islam. After their meal they all followed him to the Holy Sepulchre Church and entered through its Crusader doorways. This building raised conflicting emotions among the three Christians. According to discoveries of the Empress Helena, Christ was crucified and resurrected within its area, but it seemed doubtful to them that Christ was buried within yards of his cross; after all, the Bible spoke of Mary Magdalene and the Apostles going to a garden nearby. The church itself was not conducive to prayer, its interior divided amongst the ancient branches of the church with the Ethiopian Christians only allowed a place on the roof. Professor Mahoud and his party witnessed the constant scandal of squabbling within the church, when an Orthodox priest started having an hysterical shouting match with a cleaning woman who had trespassed on his part of the church. The Professor saw Charlotte's distress and whispered, 'This offends me as well. We believe Jesus, inshallah, was the greatest prophet before Muhammad, inshallah, and believe in Christ's Resurrection.' He collected the others and they left the church to return to his house.

When they arrived at the Professor's house they were fussed over by his wife; she had laid out a selection of pastries and very sweet cakes accompanied by mint tea. It was nearly three o'clock, but there was no sign of Rupert or the General. The imminent threat to the Dome weighed on them and the Professor showed his agitation by going into the hall and pacing up and down. They heard a vehicle screech to a stop outside, the Professor opened the front door and there was a whispered exchange. Following this an Arab figure appeared in the room where they were having tea. He was dressed in flowing robes, traditional headdress and wearing large, dark glasses. He salaamed, took off his glasses and laughed – it was Rupert. He told the men to follow him, saying, 'General Sam is outside in a small furniture van and we're going with him. I'm afraid you girls must stay here. We must leave immediately, so at the double then.'

Nicholas and Theo embraced the girls, and followed Rupert outside to see a shabby brown van, decorated by a picture of a shiny leather sofa. The engine was idling and the driver, another Arab, gestured towards the back of the van where

180

the door shutters were raised. Nicholas and Theo climbed in, but instead of joining them, Rupert closed the back, saying, 'I'm travelling up front with Sam.'

The real identity of the driver then dawned on them.

Inside the back of the van they found two Israeli soldiers, who moved to allow them to sit behind Rupert and the General, who turned round and smiled. '*Shalom*. We shall be parking near the Zion Gate so that we can observe it; already we have a number of disguised troops taking up position. When the helicopter lands, the disguised Armenian Templars will be shot as they move towards the plane, which itself will be destroyed on the ground.' He put the van into gear and they moved off, and leaving the old town took the road that circled the city walls. Ten minutes later they were parked so that they had a good view of the Zion Gate and the land in front of it. It was three-thirty. The time passed slowly. It was very hot in the van with the sun beating down on it.

Rupert stared at the city walls on either side of the gate, remembering how he used to walk on them when he was in the British Embassy and was always reminded of the city walls of York, which made him homesick for Fortesque Hall.

The General's phone kept ringing with reports from his other soldiers in their vantage points nearby. There were no signs of unusual activity and in the heat of mid-afternoon the flow of people coming out of the gate was minimal; only one Armenian priest was spotted. They heard bells telling them it was four o'clock. The General had switched on a wireless set which was reporting aircraft movements around Jerusalem. No helicopters were in the air. The General started muttering to Rupert and the others sat behind, sweating in the heat; the atmosphere became increasingly unpleasant. The General made further phone calls and then sat in silence. He looked at his watch. It was four-twenty; he turned round and said, 'I'm afraid there must have been a change of plan or your letter was mistranslated. There's no sign of any helicopter activity and nothing unusual is happening in the Armenian quarter. I shall leave a few of our disguised troops here and double forces on the Temple Mount. I'll take you back to the Professor's house; no doubt a shower and a change of clothes will be welcome.' The General's tone was gruff and Nicholas and Theo felt responsible for what appeared to be a fiasco of a false alarm.

Ten minutes later they were back at the Professor's house being offered more tea before showering and changing. The girls were relieved but also embarrassed that such elaborate Army activity had proved unnecessary. The General had driven off as soon as they reached the house, but he had given them a card with his personal and Army phone numbers.

It was nearly four-thirty when they returned to the Professor's house and as they sat round enjoying a refreshing cup of tea, a clock struck the half hour. The atmosphere was one of anti-climax and to prevent them dwelling on the fiasco of the non-event, the Professor began a didactic discussion about time. He told them Israel had four calendars in use, with its mixture of the Muslim and Jewish lunar calendars, the Julian calendar and finally the Gregorian calendar as used in the Western world; this latter calendar was the one most used but did not measure time as before Christ (BC) or Anno Domini (AD), but so as not to offend religious susceptibilities, described the years as either Before the Common Era (BCE) or present time as being during the Common Era (CE). To lighten the mood Nicholas told them of the difficulties encountered in England when they switched in the eighteenth century from the Julian lunar calendar to the solar Gregorian one. In doing so they had to adjust the date of the month by advancing it by eleven days; the population had rioted and the streets were full of cries of, 'Give us back our eleven days' – they genuinely thought they had lost eleven days of their life span. As he finished the last few words, his voice dropped to a whisper and an expression of horror appeared on his face. His friends were concerned that he might be having a heart attack, and Rupert said, 'Are you all right, old chap?'

Nicholas stood up and in a strangled voice cried out, 'No! No! I've suddenly realised what fools we've been; the time zone in Israel is one hour ahead of Switzerland, the sun getting here first.' They looked at him in amazement; he was speaking so fast it sounded gibberish. He took a deep breath. 'The invitation to Bishop Krasnos to attend the sacred ceremony today was for four o'clock, to coincide with the starting time of the Jerusalem attack, but four o'clock in Switzerland is five o'clock here so no wonder the attack didn't happen at our local time of four o'clock, but my God, it's due in twenty minutes now.'

They stood up from the table as if stung. The Professor looked at the card given him by the General and rushed to the phone and called his Army number. As it rang he handed it to Rupert, saying, 'Put him in the picture and then follow me to the back of the house.' He moved some books on the mantelpiece and pressed a red button behind them. A shrill fire bell rang at the back of the house. The Professor asked the men to follow him at once, ran down the hall and out into a courtyard at the back. He opened a shed door, moved some bric-a-brac and lifted up a floorboard revealing a stash of sub-machine guns. In answer to the fire bell two of his students ran into the courtyard from a gate at the back and were each handed a gun. The Professor gave one each to the others and, with one in his own hand, gingerly opened the gate which revealed a dingy cul-de-sac. A battered black Mercedes was parked there. The Professor yanked open the doors and gestured his guests to get in the back while he and the students jumped into the front. He revved the engine, saying, 'Put the guns on the floor and just pray there are no Israeli checkpoints.' Putting the car into gear he drove off with a scream of tyres, joined the street fronting his house and, scattering walkers, roared up to Herod's Gate at the top. Once through this, he skidded on to the ring road which skirted the Temple Mount. After a few minutes he negotiated a bend in the road as it followed the end of the Temple Mount, and they then entered the stretch of road leading to the Zion Gate – it was four-fifty. He opened the car's sliding roof and they could hear behind them the sound of an approaching helicopter. At the same time Nicholas's mobile phone rang out. It was the General.

'Where the hell are you? I gather you've left the Professor's house. I'm trying to get through the Zion Gate but I'm stuck in the Armenian quarter, behind an anti-Turkish demonstration marching through the gate. It could be a cover organised to hide the enemy in this bloody crowd until they are near the helicopter rendezvous. I only left two troops hidden in a cart near the gate, so where are you?'

Nicholas replied, 'We're just coming down the main road and can see the gate now. I hate to tell you, but there's a helicopter losing height nearby.'

The General interrupted him. 'Stay well away; there may be crossfire … ' His voice began to fade. Nicholas realised the battery on his phone was exhausted and the last words he heard were, ' … the bloody demonstration has stopped … we're stuck for the moment … '

The helicopter was now above them and appeared to be hovering as if uncertain as to where it was going to land.

21

In the Templar Castle in Switzerland the great bell in its tower began to ring at three-thirty. It issued a deep and sonorous boom and its vibrations penetrated the castle.

An hour earlier the castle had been cleared of visitors and the sixty elect members who were to attend the sacrifice had joined some forty postulants in the courtyard, where tables were spread with fine food and wine. Before they fell upon this spread the treasurer called for silence and told them to prepare for the arrival of the Grand Master. Solemn drumming commenced and the Grand Master appeared, flanked by Bishop Krasnos and Lady Natasha. The Grand Master was wearing a gold coat embroidered with signs of the zodiac. He walked to the middle of the courtyard and stood facing the assembled members of the Order. They immediately fell to their knees and bent forward until their foreheads touched the ground. The Grand Master clapped his hands three times and they all stood up. He started to speak in his deep, melodious voice.

'Today is Midsummer's Day, always of significance to our Order. We, the elect, will be offering a great sacrifice in half an hour, which will give power to an elite small band of our brethren gathering now in Jerusalem, and which will effect a significant advance in our power there. We gather here now to drink a sacred toast to their success. First we have a reluctant duty to perform ... ' Here he gave a wry smile which led to a ripple of laughter from the crowd. 'As you know, one of our members has failed grievously, one Darcy de Malplaquet, Master of the English Templars. He has failed in a critical task of eliminating a small number of our enemies, so that they remain a threat to us. He is at this moment coming here from the crypt in one of our coffins and will be lowered into the vault here. Depending on the success of our Jerusalem venture, we shall decide whether he will suffer the ultimate punishment or, if we agree to show him mercy, will be only imprisoned. So first we lower him into the vault and then you feast while we are at our sacred ceremony, after which we shall return to make our judgment. Let us now make our Midsummer toast to our Order and its success.'

A great cheer went up and four young Templar girls entered with golden flagons and began to pour generous measures into glasses set out on the tables. The drink was strong and spiced with drugs; its effect not only led to diminished self-control, but was also slightly hallucinatory. The toast was made and soon afterwards they were feeding themselves from the buffet, drinking more and kissing each other with abandon. A sound of drumming came from the corridors and the treasurer called for silence as a coffin appeared on the shoulders of six of the Indians. They marched in silence to where a gravestone had been moved, revealing the vault below. The silence was broken by the drumming of fists from within the coffin. The coffin was placed on the ground in front of the Grand Master and the lid unscrewed and removed. Manacled hands clawed the air. The Grand Master gave a signal to the Indians, who lifted up the end of the coffin and tipped it forward so that the crowd could see the dishevelled body of Malplaquet, naked save for a loincloth. Someone threw a potato from the buffet, and tomatoes and eggs followed as the crowd jeered drunkenly.

Karl was at the side of the crowd. He had not drunk the toast and he was shortly to go inside to join the young mother of his child, Regan, and with her carry it down to the crypt. The pathetic sight of Malplaquet triggered in him a remembered 'Ecce Homo' portrait of Christ. This flash of remembrance brought him close to tears. He slipped away to find his child, who was being fed by his mother; this innocent sight unsettled him still more. She was in a room overlooking the courtyard and as he entered it a great cheer came from the crowd as the coffin was being lowered into its grave. Karl had prepared a bassinet to carry the baby down to the crypt. It was time to go, and as he went over to take the baby, its mother began crying. He laid the baby in its cot and went over to the young Regan, saying, 'I've arranged something with the Grand Master. The baby won't be killed, but like Abraham we shall be seen to be offering our son for sacrifice. I shall make a dramatic signal and then hand the baby to you. You must stand close to the altar and then run as fast as you can up and out of the crypt. We are promised a great reward.'

Regan's face lit up with joy and she came over to Karl and kissed him. 'I knew and prayed you would save the three of us.' She began to cry again and then went to pick up the bassinet before Karl could get to it. She cried out, 'What on earth is in here? It weighs a ton!'

Karl laughed. 'Don't worry; it's all to do with the Abraham surprise. Let me carry it. We must be on our way to the crypt.'

Once there, Karl put the bassinet behind the altar and then joined the queue to collect the robes for himself and Regan before changing.

The crypt was filling with incense, a mixture of a musky scent with that of cannabis, making visibility almost impossible as the only illumination came from the sanctuary lamps and large black candles on the surrounding altars. A musical background was provided by two drummers, a trumpeter and a player of wailing pipes of Pan. A roll of drums and a short trumpet fanfare heralded the start of the ceremony. The Grand Master, Bishop Krasnos and Lady Natasha entered, but this time in black copes; the Grand Master and the Bishop were wearing goat-like masks and

Natasha one of a cat. They walked towards the altar, their copes swinging open to display their nakedness. The Bishop led the Grand Master to sit in front of the altar on a gold-painted throne. He then took from the altar two diamond-encrusted, gold chalices; one was filled with the elixir of life and the other with a hallucinogenic liqueur; the latter he gave to Lady Natasha and together they moved into the circle of Templars now surrounding the altar. They dispensed a single sip to each of the worshippers. The pipes of Pan and a slow beat of the drum timed the movements of the Templars who had now formed two circles; the inner circle of women faced outwards towards the second circle of men. The trumpet sounded and the Grand Master stood up and went behind the altar. The candlelight illuminated a glinting curved dagger held in both his hands. He gestured to Karl to join him and together they moved forward a few inches from the altar. Bishop Krasnos joined them, holding the prayer book brought by the Russian from Rasputin's library. The Bishop began to read the ritual in a staccato rhythm of some Slavonic language. Every few minutes they stopped and the trumpet sounded a long, wailing note, followed by a roll of the drums. The third time this happened the assembly began to chant repeatedly, 'Hail Bahomet, our sacrifice is here,' each time punctuated by the drums and the shrill pipes of Pan.

The Grand Master turned to Karl. 'Present our sacrifice!'

Karl moved to Regan and took their child and handed it to the Grand Master, who held it high in the air above the altar; the baby began to scream in distress. The Grand Master lowered him into the basin-like depression on top of the altar. Underneath it Natasha had already slipped on to the mattress below. The Grand Master's mouth was wet with saliva, his eyes half closed in a drug-induced ecstasy. He turned to Karl and in a loud voice shouted out, 'The sacrifice will be greater if the father makes it.' He handed the dagger to Karl; his face was distorted with an expression of lustful expectancy. He bent forward and raised the head of the baby. 'Now the sacrifice,' he commanded and, turning to Karl, hissed, 'Slit the throat and I shall elevate the baby for all to see.' He seemed to be in a mad delirium; his eyes were rolling and his mouth was flecked with spittle.

The drums, the trumpet and the pipes of Pan screamed out a cacophony of confused sound. The Grand Master glared at Karl, and again he hissed, 'Slit its throat!'

Karl gripped the dagger and followed the Grand Master's command and using all his force sliced through the wind pipe, but not the baby's throat, the Grand Master's! The dying Grand Master slumped forward, blood spurting from his wound; the baby was snatched away by Karl. There was a stunned silence except for obscene moaning from below the altar. Karl ran and gave the baby to its mother, Regan, who ran for the stairs as he had commanded. As quick as a flash Karl went to the bassinet and picked up from under the mattress a machine gun and two grenades.

'Get back,' he shouted, as a small group began to move towards him. He sprayed the stone floor with bullets, which sent up shards of stone. The advancing men fell back, knocking over the women behind them. Karl fired again and panic gripped them as they turned and tried to run towards the cloakrooms. Karl ran backwards towards the stairs, firing short bursts from the machine gun. As he gained height he heard the heavy thud of a thrown candlestick hit the stairs beside him and growing shouts of rage. In their drugged state, the Templars were coming after him. He stopped and pulled the pin out of one of the grenades and lobbed it towards his pursuers. He had just passed the window looking into the depths of the moat, and the grenade bounced down the steps and on to the windowsill. Karl went on slipping and stumbling forward up the stairs. He stopped again and fired a further burst from the machine gun. The sound of the ascending Templars stopped; Karl resumed his ascent and reached the open door leading into the chapel. At that very moment there was an explosion from the grenade below and its blast threw him on to the floor of the chapel. It also blasted out the glass of the window looking into the waters of the moat; a surge of water exploded through the four-foot window and swept the stunned pursuers down into the crypt. There was no other exit for those below and in a few seconds a foot of water was rising in powerful surges around the crypt. Some of those trapped tried to climb through the torrent to escape up the stairs, but it was too powerful and they were swept back. Ten minutes later there was no more life in the crypt.

Master Karl disappeared with Regan and their child to a small farm he had secretly bought near Appenzel. Before they left the Castle he had dashed to the Grand Master's office, where he knew an elaborately bound address book was kept. He had a desperate need to find out the address of the Abbey of Samouz so that they could continue to enjoy the elixir of life. Karl managed to find the address, but unfortunately it was only a box number. He made it his most urgent priority to find out where it was.

22

At the same time as the Grand Master of the Templars fell dead, the traffic on the main road leading to the Zion Gate in Jerusalem came to a halt. The low-flying helicopter had distracted an approaching lorry driver and a head-on collision occurred two hundred yards ahead of the Professor's car. An urgent discussion began in the front of the Professor's Mercedes; the young men picked their submachines guns off the floor and rested them upright between their knees so that they pointed in the air through the open roof. They could see a long procession coming out of the Zion Gate, at the front of which people were waving placards and chanting slogans. The Professor turned round and told the others to get their guns ready, pointing through the roof in the same way as those of the students; if they saw the helicopter land the Professor said he would drive on to the ground by the side of the road and get as near as he could so that they could shoot down anyone dressed as an Armenian priest running towards the plane. It seemed that only they could now save the Dome of the Rock. The helicopter was moving from side to side over the open ground.

Theo turned to Rupert. 'How do we fire this bloody thing? I assume there's a safety catch to move before we squeeze the trigger.'

Rupert showed him where it was and Theo moved it back and forth. The helicopter was drifting sideways over the stalled traffic; there was a strong crosswind. The Professor kept cursing the unmoving traffic and the helicopter was circling again, gradually losing height and now hovering fifty feet in front of them, throwing up clouds of dust from the parched ground. The Professor started sounding his horn, wrenched the steering wheel to the right and revved the engine. By mistake he engaged the gears and the car shot forward, mounting the side of the road to bump along the rough ground until they were enveloped in the dust cloud created by the helicopter, now above them. The Professor, unable to see clearly, hit a rock and the car shuddered over it and stopped so suddenly that everyone in the car was thrown about like toys. Theo lurched forward and squeezed the trigger of his sub-machine gun; mistakenly he had left the safety catch in the fire position so that a stream of bullets soared into the air through the open car roof.

'Drunken Dionysus,' shouted Theo.

The others stared at him, aghast. They looked up through the dust cloud, now thinning, and saw that Theo had shot off the steering propeller at the rear of the helicopter, bits of which crashed around them and on to the bonnet of the car. The helicopter veered to the right over the open ground and then, in seeming panic, shot upwards; the whole of its body was spinning slowly in a circle around its large surviving propeller, which could merely give it lift.

Rupert seized Theo's gun, sank back in the seat of the car and burst into a roar of laughter. Tears of uncontrolled merriment began to run down his cheeks.

'Good shot, Theo the Greek! Oh my sainted aunt, you've immobilised the bloody enemy. There's no way that's going to the Dome of the Rock!'

They were all seized with uncontrollable laughter, all except Theo, who sat in a state of shock, mouth open, but unable to say a word.

The helicopter climbed up even higher. The procession had cleared the Zion Gate and out of it two Armenian priests began to run towards the point below the helicopter. Shortly afterwards another appeared, running more slowly, and carrying a holdall. The Professor shouted in Arabic to his young companions. They leapt out of the car and ran towards the Armenians, their guns at the ready. The disguised priests were throwing off their robes so that they could run faster, revealing Israeli Army uniforms beneath them, so that when they bombed the Dome, it would be falsely blamed on the Israeli Army. The helicopter began to descend and they could see the pilot gesticulating at them to go away. At the same time an Arab standing by a mule cart, parked by the side of the road leading to the Zion Gate, rushed to the back of the cart and pulled back a tarpaulin. It revealed two Israeli soldiers quickly getting into position behind a mounted machine gun; they shouted a command for the running figures to stop. It was ignored and the machine gun sprayed a stream of fire a foot above the ground, felling the running figures. An armoured car and an Army ambulance appeared through the Zion Gate; the procession was now through it. The General was in the armoured car, which left the road and bumped along the rough ground with the ambulance following it to stop by the wounded bombers. Above them smoke began to appear around the shot-off rear propeller of the helicopter. The pilot wisely decided to land under control rather than crash. The Professor, seeing they had no further part to play, shouted to his companions and they ran back to his Mercedes. He opened the boot, collected the guns from the others and hid them under a collection of vegetables and dog blankets. Rupert, Nicholas and Theo had left the car, uncertain as to what they could do. The Professor shooed them back into the car. The traffic was moving again, so he backed the car towards the main road. Along it a stream of Army vehicles appeared and blocked any further movement by the Professor. Troops poured out of them and advanced to surround the helicopter and the wounded enemy. The Templars, weapons had slipped from their reach after their legs were hit, and most importantly the holdall containing the bomb was left standing away from its carrier.

The General had leapt out of his armoured car and was in his element, directing the bomb disposal experts and the collection of the wounded Templars. Coming over to the lorries that had unloaded the troops, the General saw the Professor and the others in his car. Already the General had been told that the helicopter had been demobilised by shots coming from an unknown direction; seeing the Professor and the occupants of his car, he quickly realised where they had come from. As they saw the General approaching, they leapt out of their car and the General embraced Rupert and warmly shook the others' hands.

The General smiled broadly. 'Thank goodness I had left two of my soldiers in that mule cart and that we were able to warn them when you discovered the true timing.' He began to laugh, and slapped Rupert on the back. 'Wonderful shooting by my men, crippling the helicopter.' He winked at them and added, 'By the way, when I was stuck in the Armenian quarter, I had a call from one Captain Patricia of British Intelligence – she was concerned for your safety, as well she might have been. She was talking from Switzerland and told me to tell you the Swiss police were moving to arrest all the Templars in their Castle. She's now getting a plane from Zurich to Tel Aviv and bringing with her the new head of her section, a Lieutenant General Maitland, so that tomorrow we can share information on the Templars. I've booked them in to the King David Hotel. We want you, plus the Professor, to join us there for a debriefing. Ten in the morning, prompt.' He turned away, and waving goodbye, ran over at the double to the helicopter, where its pilot was being searched.

The jubilant Professor rang his wife and told her to pass on the good news to Charlotte and Kirsten. The Army vehicles blocking him moved away and he was able to get back on to the road. With flashing lights and the hooting of his horn, he made a U-turn and sped back towards his home, shouting praises to Muhammad.

Later, washed and changed, they all went with the Professor and his students up to the Dome of the Rock for evening prayers to give thanks for its deliverance. There had been a brief report on the television about a military action near the Zion Gate, but no reason for it was given. When they left the mosque, there was a crowd of some fifty students. As the Professor and his party came down the steps, the students surged around them, shaking their hands, raising their fists in the air and shouting triumphantly. The two young men who had been in the car had obviously spread the news.

A cry went up, 'Where is the mighty destroyer of helicopters? Where is the Greek? Three cheers for Theo the Greek!' Other visitors to the Temple Mount gathered round in interest and the tale of their triumph spread. A small team of cameramen appeared, and a reporter with a microphone started to interview the Professor, who gave a highly edited version of events.

'No! They were not Hamas, but we were passing by on our way to shoot wild dogs in the Hinom Valley and, realising that the helicopter was a threat, got our best shot, Theo, to immobilise it. Simple as that.'

The students had other ideas and, taking them by their arms, told them a celebration party awaited them. The Professor seemed to be known by all of them and Rupert, Theo and Nicholas were carried triumphantly, shoulder high, while the girls followed alongside relishing the fun. They continued in good spirits to the party, where speeches, dancing and good food helped to dull the tension of the day. Once in bed they slept like logs.

It was more by luck than efficiency that they arrived at the King David Hotel in time for their ten o'clock meeting next day. They had agreed to let the Professor take the lead in describing to the General why they had rushed to the Zion Gate, with only hunting rifles. The General had looked at the ceiling and smiled wryly while this explanation was given, knowing full well that more powerful weaponry had been used, no doubt courtesy of Hamas. He saw no virtue in questioning their obvious possession of automatic weapons when they had prevented a Middle East disaster.

Before the meeting broke up, Captain Patricia appeared and introduced them all to her new head of section, Lieutenant General Maitland, and was able to tell them the news that when the police arrived at the castle in Zurzach they found only forty distressed and bewildered young postulant Templars, none of whom told them about the crypt. It was only days later that it was discovered and the dead removed.

They moved on after their meeting to a convivial lunch in the hotel and the General was able to tell them that the President of Israel had been fully informed and that he had just been told that a reception with the President was being arranged for that evening. The President would be awarding them each a medal as honoured friends of Israel. The British Ambassador would also be attending. It had been agreed that no one would mention the involvement of the Templars, but just that they had foiled a terrorist plot to destroy the Dome of the Rock. Unfortunately they could not escape the attentions of the media.

The following morning the Master of Michaelhouse choked on his toast as he read the newspapers, which were pictures of the young heroic don of his College, Nicholas. It was also reported that he hoped to marry in the College chapel a young Newnham postgraduate, Charlotte Fox, who had also been involved in foiling this international plot.

In Harvard, the US newspapers, as usual, contained little foreign news and the matter was not reported until a week later, when TV news stations began to show pictures of the students rejoicing outside the Dome of the Rock.

For the time being the Templar cult faded away and the young postulants left were taken into various mental care institutions until cured of their delusions.

At the President's reception in Jerusalem, Theo and Kirsten announced that they too were engaged to be married. The engagements of the four were greeted with further delight by the media and pictures of them together were circulated worldwide, especially by two magazines, *Hello* and *OK*, neither of which had previously featured in their reading lists.

Returning to their normal lives, their traumas were healed by the preparations for their respective marriages and they quickly retreated from the modern world into that of their historical studies, from which they hoped not to be disturbed again. That hope, however, depended on no further madness infecting the world from the hidden Abbey of Somouz, from which the power of the elixir of life and the questionable possession of the Holy Grail still constituted a dangerous threat to the world.